Fletcher's FLAME

Fletcher's Flame

BY

LEXI POST

Fletcher's Flame:

Last Chance Series, Book 3

By Lexi Post

Can he get her to see her own worth before they both go up in flames…literally?

Dana Wilson has one mission in life – to save animals. Thanks to her life's calling, she's developed a distrust of men in authority. So when Bo Fletcher, a cowboy firefighter, decides to appoint himself her bodyguard, her hackles rise.

Bo's physical attraction to Dana Wilson has him digging deeper into her personality, a need to understand her burning in his gut. Unfortunately, that's not the only thing burning. An arsonist appears to be nipping at Dana's heels and Bo is determined to protect her.

As sparks fly between them, the fires come closer and closer to claiming Dana. Can Bo protect her or will his own words be her demise?

Acknowledgments

To Bob Fabich Sr., my hot, real-life Fire Chief. Thank you for helping me with all my fire details. Any incorrect information regarding fires and investigation are fictitious for the sake of the story. And for my sister Paige Wood who improves my work every time with her observations.

Bette Read, thank you for telling me all about Ruby Ranch in Phoenix and all the wonderful work they do. It was the inspiration for my Rainbow Acres Refuge. If anyone is looking for a pet that needs a forever home, please contact them. They have a great core of volunteers that will help get the animal to you http:// www.rubyranchrescue.org/

Of course, I couldn't send this story out the door without my awesome critique partner, Marie Patrick, giving it her love and attention. Nor could I let my baby go into the world without my wonderful pre-pub team. Thank you KC Crocker, Lisa Guertin, Marianne Hughes, Karen Roma and Pamela Todd.

This story is dedicated to Digger, a very special

bearded dragon, who crossed the rainbow bridge way before her momma was ready to lose her.

Thank you to Paige Tyler for granting permission for the use of the characters of Lexi Fletcher, Dane Chandler, Captain Earl Stewart, Tory Wilcox, Nate Boone and Jax Malloy from her Dallas Fire & Rescue Series world.

Author's Note

Fletcher's Flame was inspired by Bret Harte's short story, *Mliss*, published in 1869. Mliss is the daughter of the drunk founding father of a small western town. She is odd according to her peers. Even the school teacher, who she tells she wants "learning," isn't sure what to make of her, but he lets her attend the one room school house anyway. It turns out she is quite bright, and despite her father's suicide, she begins to gain respect for her intelligence, if not for her ladylike comportment. She doesn't try to be like the other girls and knows what she wants out of life.

Eventually, the teacher decides to take a new job in a new town and Mliss finds out before he can tell her. She feels betrayed and plans to leave town with a traveling band of actors. The teacher is outraged that she would risk her life by leaving with the actors and saves her from her fate.

But what if she equates all authority figures with her father and won't accept the protection she needs? What would it take to get through to her that she is worth so much more than she realizes even after being betrayed again?

Chapter One

Dana Wilson moaned as the smoke alarm blared from her ceiling. Really? She'd just put new batteries in that stupid thing. Pulling the pillow over her head, she tried to keep out the sound.

"Ugh." Lifting up one side, she peeked at the clock. 3:17 a.m. She had to get up in two more hours. Frustrated, she took a deep breath.

She sniffed. *Was that smoke? Crapola on a bun, it is!*

What an idiot! Whipping off the covers, she swung her feet down and into her slippers, her long t-shirt twisting up to bare her ass. A shout came from below.

High pitched whining followed by someone running down the hall upstairs made it clear her apartment building was on fire. The three story building was at least a hundred years old, one of the reasons she moved into it, but it would go up like a tinder box.

Stay calm. Nothing ever came of panicking. It's no different than the time you were on that cliff with the baby deer.

She turned on her lamp before running through her bedroom. As she rounded the corner into her tiny vestibule, she hit her bare thigh on the small table against the wall. *Stupid thing.* Rubbing her leg, she finally reached her apartment door. She unlocked both locks and pulled it open.

Smoke billowed in, smothering all her senses before she slammed the door shut, coughing as the foreign matter filled her lungs. *Not good.*

Quickly, she ran into the kitchen, grabbed the hand towel and soaked it with water. She brought it to her face and hurried back to her door.

Here goes nothing.

As she opened the door, smoke streamed in and she dropped into a crouch. *Stay low. Remember the barn fire in Maryland. Smoke rises.* After the initial billow, she found she could stand without too much smoke. Looking up, she froze.

Hell. I'm in hell. Black smoke covered the hallway ceiling, billowing like an upside down wave, slowly lowering. Yellow flickers lit it sporadically like heat lightning in the clouds on a summer evening.

"Get out of my way." Randal who lived in 204 pushed by her, his Chihuahua in his arms as he headed for the stairs.

"Excuse me." She yelled as she turned to follow him.

She glanced across the hallway making out the numbers 202 through the thickening haze. Surely Tanya had made it out. Unable to leave without checking, she stepped across the small hallway and banged on the door. "Tanya, wake up!" She tried the door but it was locked.

Her neighbor must have left already. Or she could be at her latest boyfriend's house.

"Help! Help us!" At the sound of yelling coming from behind her, her blood ran cold. Holy moly, the Sheridans were still in their apartment!

She looked longingly at the stairs not twenty feet away, but turned her back on them. The smoke hung lower and she bent over to avoid the worst of it.

Now she truly walked toward the gates of hell. At the end of the hall, where an old couch sat was the inferno. Flames reached up the wall and toward the ceiling, licking their way closer to her neighbors' door.

"Somebody help us!" The high pitched yell had to be Mrs. Sheridan.

Dana wiped at her eyes with her wet towel, or rather damp towel. Then she took a breath into it and removed it from her mouth. "Mrs. Sheridan! Unlock your door!"

"We're in here!" The high pitched voice came closer. "We're in here!"

She moved along the wall between her apartment and the Sheridans'. The old three story building had never been renovated, so despite the blaring smoke alarms, there were no automatic sprinklers to slow down the fire.

The flames moved closer to the opposite side of the Sheridans' door from her. If she was actually going to help, she had to do it now. She banged on the door. "Hurry! Open the door!"

The sound of fire engine sirens drowned out her words.

"Please help us!"

Her pulse raced so fast, she was surprised she remained conscious. The heat from the fire was worse than a Dallas sidewalk in August and it seemed to billow towards her. *It's now or never.* She grabbed the doorknob.

The sirens stopped. *They must be here.* She could let them do their job. But even as the thought crossed her mind, she turned the knob.

As the door swung open, Mrs. Sheridan screamed.

Just like with her own apartment, black smoke poured in and she ran in after it. "Come on, you have to leave now." She pointed back behind her.

Mr. Sheridan rose from his recliner, the chair creaking as he lifted his bulk from it. He coughed as he reached his height, breathing in the black smoke. "Is that what the firefighters said?"

He never believed she knew anything even when she was proven right, so she lied. "Yes, they said we were to leave immediately."

The man raised one brow in doubt.

Really? His front door was on fire and he expected the firefighters to say stay inside?

"I told you, sweetie." Mrs. Sheridan coughed daintily. "Please can we go now?" The elderly woman was as thin and petite as her husband was heavy and large. She never did anything without his approval, and he rarely gave his approval.

"You want to go through that?" He pointed toward the open door.

One side of the door jamb was lit with small flames. How did firefighters get through to people like this? "Yes, because if you wait any longer, the whole door will be filled with fire and you'll be stuck in here and eventually the floor will give way and you'll burn to death."

Mrs. Sheridan gasped then proceeded to choke on the contaminated air.

Maybe she'd laid it on a little thick, but at least she got her point across. Mr. Sheridan actually moved, right past his wife, bumping into her as he lumbered toward the exit.

Dana squelched her instinctive retort and instead grasped Mrs. Sheridan by the arm and guided her out, pulling her lower to avoid the descending smoke. As they entered the hall, a figure appeared at the top of the stairs. The bulky outline told her a fire firefighter had arrived.

A surge of relief ran through her until another man appeared behind him. She tried to swallow, but her throat was raw from the smoke and her dry dishtowel was technically worthless.

The second firefighter had to be almost seven feet tall and his shoulders looked four feet wide. He carried a huge ax making him appear even more impressive. She squinched her eyes in a fruitless effort to stop them from watering. Holy moly, the man was a giant! *It's just a firefighter like the one who helped you get out of the barn with Wind Dancer last year—*

Hell and damnation. "Mrs. Sheridan, where's Misty?"

The older woman shook her head, her focus on the approaching giant. The other firefighter had already begun to guide Mr. Sheridan down the stairs.

There was no way she would leave the cat behind. As the giant reached them, she pushed Mrs. Sheridan at him. "Here, take her." She doubted he could hear her, her voice raspy in her own ears, but it didn't matter.

She turned quickly.

"Stop! Come back!"

The command in his voice had her halting instinctively, but she forced herself to run away from him and the safety he represented. She couldn't count on them to save Misty.

She thought he swore, but she couldn't be sure as she made it to the Sheridans' doorway. The entire door was now on fire, flames starting to lick the walls inside.

She still held the towel over her nose and mouth, even though it did little to keep the smoke from scratching at her throat like a frightened cat. Misty had to be scared to death.

Where would I hide if I was a cat? She ran to the Sheridans' bedroom, the smoke not quite as heavy, and flipped the switch. The overhead light came on, but flickered. Dropping to her knees, she looked under the bed.

Glowing eyes met her gaze and her heart cried. The

white Persian was petrified. It lay near the head of the bed, its whole body scrunched against the wall.

"It's okay, Misty. I'm going to get you out of here. Can you help me do that?" She'd never had a frightened cat help her save it. Never. So she didn't wait for that.

Instead, she stood and threw her useless towel on the bed. Grasping the headboard, she pushed with all her might and it moved away from the wall.

Luckily, the cat remained where she was, but Dana still couldn't reach her.

Walking to the other side of the bed, she heaved again. That proved successful, but she had to stop as a coughing fit took her. *Stupid smoke.*

After she stopped choking, she wiped her eyes. When she could finally see again, the cat was gone.

Really? I don't expect a rescue to go smoothly, but it would be nice if one thing went right.

Dropping to the floor again, she looked under the bed.

Misty looked back at her without blinking.

How did cats do that, especially in all this smoke? She didn't hesitate. This was a familiar scenario. Looking around the room for anything long, she found a cane and grabbed it. Getting on the exit side of the bed, she swept the cane under it toward Misty, forcing the kitty toward her.

Misty walked from beneath the bed slowly, and as soon as she wasn't pushed anymore, promptly lay down again.

Smart cat. The heavy smoke was almost as low as the top of the bed. Luckily, on the floor, breathing was a tad easier.

Dana moved slowly, keeping the cane where it was so the cat couldn't scoot back under the bed while she kept her body between it and the door to the living room. As her right hand grasped the back of the cat's neck, the light went out.

That couldn't be good. Pulling the struggling cat into her arms, she took a minute to assess her position.

It wasn't the first time she'd rescued an animal in a dangerous situation, nor was it her first fire. She tried not to think of her few belongings going up in smoke. She'd become used to living with very few personal items since she was a child, so she wasn't attached to most of her things. Life was much more precious, especially that in her arms.

She kissed the top of the cat's head then wiped her mouth on her sleeve—the cat's fur was covered in dust. Crawling on all fours wouldn't be easy with Misty, but it was their best chance for getting out of the building.

Scooting over to a dresser near the doorway, she opened the bottom drawer and pulled out what looked like a summer housecoat. Carefully, she wrapped it around her and tied it in front of her to hold the cat. Unfortunately, it probably left her backside bare since all she had on was her extra-large t-shirt and slippers, but her dress wasn't her priority.

With the cat secured, she crawled into the living room and stopped as she stared at the door to the hall. It was now completely engulfed in flames.

Crap. Crap. Crap.

She coughed as the smoke filled her lungs again and Misty squirmed in her cocoon.

Sorry sweetie, but you need to stay with me.

Water. Water put out fire. She had to get water. *Oh, a wet blanket!*

Moving into the bedroom again, she pulled the summer blanket off the bed and crawled with it to the bathroom. Turning the shower on she managed to get the blanket into it and pulled it over herself.

She crawled back to the living room, her progress slow as fits of coughing made her stop. She checked on Misty and the cat appeared sluggish. No more squirming.

Come on Misty, don't give up yet.

She drew closer to the door, wishing the paper thin wall between her apartment and the Sheridans' really was paper thin, but it wasn't. The old building may be worn, but it was well built.

She stopped before the flaming doorway. She thought she'd seen hell earlier, but this looked seriously demonic. Could she crawl through and then…and then, what would she do then?

Did it matter? Hell was waiting for her. She moved one knee forward but coughing stopped her. She had to get out. She had to save Misty.

When her coughing stopped, she checked Misty, rubbing the cat's head. There was no response. Her eyes welled with tears. *Please Misty. You have to make it.*

She wiped her face with the wet blanket then tried breathing in it. It was too thick, so she pulled it away. Maybe the firefighters would put the fire out. Then she and Misty would be all right.

You're losing it.

She lifted her head and stared at the flames. Maybe she could make a run for it. She coughed even as she took a breath. Her muscles weakened as she tried to fill her lungs with oxygen. She couldn't stay on her hands and knees anymore.

She rolled to her side and cradled Misty. *We're going to get out of this, sweetie. I promise.*

Another coughing fit caught her up and she tried desperately to breathe, but it was no use. Everything went from gray to black.

Bo guided the older woman outside, keeping his grip gentle even though every muscle in his body was tense.

Tenants from the building gathered on the opposite side of the street, but they weren't all out yet. He'd never lost a person in a burning building and even though he was only on loan to the station for a month, he wasn't about to start now.

He walked the frail lady toward the paramedics. "Why did that woman run back into your apartment?"

The lady looked confused at first, her gaze on her husband who was being helped onto a gurney by Rick. Finally, she focused on him. "Oh, she went back for Misty."

Misty? There was another woman in the building? Bo pressed his radio button. "Rick, there's two more."

The firefighter he'd been partnered with jogged over to him, and without a word, they both ran back into the building.

A one-and-a-half-inch hose was being pulled up the stairs, even as he and Rick ran up behind them. "Misty!" He hoped to hear some kind of response. He should have asked the frail lady which apartment the two women might be in.

The water started and smoke obliterated all sight. He pressed his radio. "I'll take the apartment on the left."

"I've got the one across the hall." Rick's voice reassured him they had the apartments closest to the fire first.

Feeling his way along the wall, he found a flaming doorway. "Need water over here!"

The men on the hose moved the stream of water to the door, effectively squelching the flames. The smoke billowed out again as they moved back to the base of the fire along the back wall.

Bo didn't wait for the smoke to clear away. "Misty! Misty!"

When there was no response, his stomach tightened. She had to be here somewhere. He moved forward blindly, the fresh smoke making it impossible to see…and breathe if anyone was in the apartment.

His heart started to race even as his foot hit something soft on the floor. He dropped to a crouch and found a body. No! No bodies on his watch! Dropping his ax, he felt for a face.

The smoke rose, giving him a visual. A blanket practically smothered the person on the floor, and he whipped it aside. Long dark hair fell on one side of the woman in a fetal position. Her arms were wrapped around the bulge of her stomach.

Pregnant. Great. So much for an over-the-shoulder carry. He should grab her under her arms and drag her out, but one look at her bare legs and ass had him nixing that idea. He pressed his radio button. "I've got a pregnant woman. Coming out."

He sat her up to move one arm behind her back. He wriggled one arm beneath her knees and rose. She wasn't the heaviest thing he'd lifted, but with fifty-four pounds of fire gear on, she definitely challenged him.

He quickly headed out, carefully maneuvering them both through the smoking doorway and into the hall.

Rick met him there and spoke without the radio. "I searched all three apartments, there was no one else. Are you sure there were two?"

He shook his head. "No. I only saw one, but was told she'd gone in for another. I found this one in the first room. There might be another further in."

Rick nodded. "I'll check."

"I need to get her out."

"Go ahead. We've got it under control now. I'll make them stay until I come out." Rick patted him on the back and headed into the apartment.

Bo started down the stairs, hoping there was no one back there. He hated the idea of anyone not making it.

He exited the building and made a beeline for the ambulance. Two paramedics steadied a gurney as he gently laid the woman on it. One of them was his cousin Lexi, who'd transferred to Station 58 not long ago. Quickly, she threw a blanket over the woman's bare, soot covered legs and covered her mouth with oxygen.

He should go back and help Rick search for Misty, but he needed to know this victim would make it.

Lexi cut the flowered clothing from around her patient and a white ball of fur slid off. His cousin caught it and turned to him with a smirk. "We've got her, Bo, but you might want to take care of this." She deposited the limp figure in his hand.

Chapter Two

A cat? She wasn't pregnant? Damn. Bo strode to Engine 82 and pulled an infant oxygen mask from a compartment before he held it over the cat's face. He massaged the animal's dirty tummy with one of his fingers.

Irritation at the woman brewed. She could have been killed. For a cat.

Rick's voice came over the radio. "No one else on the second floor."

Relieved but puzzled, he focused on bringing the cat to consciousness. In the back of his practical mind was the unrealistic belief that if he could bring the cat back, his cousin could bring the woman back. She must have loved this cat to have risked her life to save it. He didn't want to be the one to tell her it didn't make it.

He continued to work on the ball of dirty white fur, pressing its little chest in quick rhythm. "Come on, kitty. Your mom needs you."

Bo looked at Trent and Lexi, who still surrounded the woman he'd pulled out. Then they rolled the gurney to the ambulance and hoisted it in. She was bound to have lung damage. Shit.

Rick approached, pulling his SCBA off. He stared at the small bundle in his arms. "What you got?"

He grimaced. "Cat."

Rick shook his head as if he thought the animal was a lost cause.

Bo didn't consider himself overly obsessed with animals, but this time he needed this cat to live. Ignoring Rick's obvious prognosis, he continued to tend to the kitty.

The cat's paws started to twitch and relief surged through him. As superstitious as the next firefighter, he read the cat's movement as a sign the woman would live.

He lifted the mask away for a moment to see if the kitty had its eyes open. It didn't. Moving his hand to cover the cat's face again with the oxygen, his gaze caught a small shiny tag on the animal's collar. He flicked it with his finger.

"Misty."

More relief came as he replaced the oxygen mask over Misty's face. Now at least he knew for sure there was no one else on the second floor of the old building. All four apartments were clear. He should probably get the animal to a vet soon.

How could she risk her life for her cat? He had to be thankful she hadn't endangered anyone else besides herself. Still, the thought that she might not make it because she loved her animal so much, twisted his gut.

"Misty!" The frail woman he'd helped out of the building earlier came toward him, her hands clasped together in front of her. "I thought I'd never see her again."

He frowned at the woman. "This is *your* cat?"

She nodded, tears in her eyes. "My husband told me to leave it. Thank you so much for saving her. When Dana went back for her, I thought I'd never see her again."

Bo's anger over the woman named Dana risking her life for someone else's animal made him even more uncomfortable than taking credit for something he didn't do. "I just gave it oxygen. Your neighbor found your cat." If he called the cat by its name, it just might put him over the edge. Of all the stupid, asinine things to do while a fire was eating away at—

"She'll be alright, won't she?" The frail woman looked at him with fear. "I couldn't lose her."

He had to switch his focus from the woman on her way to the hospital even now to the cat in his arms. Didn't anyone in that building understand that human life took priority?

He looked down at the furball in the crook of his arm and took away the mask. The cat's light-blue eyes stared back at him like a deer in headlights. "I think she'll be okay." He lowered the mask again. "But you'll need to bring your cat to a vet."

The woman looked toward the ambulance that housed her husband.

That it hadn't left the scene like the other one told him the man's injuries weren't serious. He pushed aside his brewing anger at the uncertain look in the fragile woman's eyes. "Ma'am, would you like an officer to bring you and your cat to an emergency vet clinic?"

The woman tore her gaze from the ambulance. "I'm not sure. My husband—"

"Will be fine." In fact, he wouldn't be surprised to hear the man had exaggerated his condition. Any man that leaves a burning building before his wife is a loser. He took the mask away from the cat and it opened its mouth, but no sound came out. "Here. Take your kitty, and I'll have someone take you to a vet."

The woman cradled her cat in her arms where the animal actually appeared to relax.

He guided her to a female officer and explained the situation. Luckily, the officer was very sympathetic and ushered the frail woman to her cruiser. He opened the door and helped her in, cat and all. He kept the door open and leaned down. "Can you tell me Dana's last name?"

The woman smiled. "Of course. That's Dana Wilson. She's an angel. I'm going to make her a big pan of lasagna just as soon as I get back home." The woman's gaze shifted to the now smoldering building. "If I still have one."

He gave her a sympathetic grin. "That you and your loved ones got out alive is most important."

She nodded and smiled at her cat. "Thank you again for saving Misty. If it weren't for you and Dana, I know I would have lost her." She looked up at him with tears making their way down her face. "If there is ever anything I can do for you, just let me know. I'm Mrs. Sheridan."

He swallowed. It was like watching a mother with her baby. "Take care of yourself." He closed the door quickly and stepped back as the cruiser pulled away from the curb.

Dana Wilson and he had a very important conversation coming about not running back into burning buildings. He took a shaky breath. If she still lived.

His gut clenched. It was more than simply his record of not losing a single person. It was about human life. He hated that fire could take it in such an agonizing way.

Even as the image of his best friend writhing in agony began to fill his head, he shut it down and strode toward the fire engine.

As Bo reached it, Cole Hatcher pulled up in his truck. He and Cole used to run into each other on the rodeo circuit when they were younger, when they thought they could master any bull.

Then a particular bull named Hades sent them both to the hospital for a week, where they shared the same room, and they'd become friends. He liked to believe he'd given Cole the idea to become a firefighter since it had been his plan since he was eight.

He grabbed a water bottle and chugged half of it down before Cole reached him. He'd liked Cole from the start. Easy going, played by the rules, and as big as he was. Cole was the only person he felt normal next to, as opposed to being the giant in the room. His friend owned a horse rescue ranch in Arizona but was in town for arson school. They'd reconnected over a few beers and a Rangers game a couple nights earlier.

"Hey Fletch. Guess you've got a possible arson here."

"We do?" He hadn't paid much attention to the fire's behavior. His sole purpose was to rescue anyone inside.

"Yeah, your captain called it in and my trainer sent me to shadow the fire investigator. All part of arson school."

"Well, I hope they have better luck with this one. The last arson case, they couldn't prove the guy had burned his building down for the insurance money. They could prove it was arson, but they couldn't determine whether it was him or his biggest competitor."

Cole nodded. "They couldn't convict based on doubt, right?"

He nodded. "Luckily with that one, it was a business and no one was in the building at the time."

His friend moved his gaze to the apartment house and then to the remaining ambulance. "I take it there were people in this one?"

"People, animals, prized possessions, everything."

"Damn, that sucks."

"Yeah." He and Cole stood in silence for a moment watching the men pull the one-and-a-half-inch hose out of the building. "What's weird is the fire started on the second floor. Why not the first floor?"

Cole chuckled. "You sure you don't want to become an arson investigator, too?"

He took another swallow of water. "No, thank you. I'd rather save lives and douse fires than pour over details after the fact."

"I get that. But where I'm from, the towns are so small we need someone to be trained in this." Cole shrugged. "It doesn't hurt that it comes with a pay raise and I'll still be fighting fires."

"Not here." Bo nodded toward the street. "We have a huge crew in the Dallas Fire and Rescue department. Everyone has a specialty. Mine is saving people."

"Did you save anyone tonight?"

He nodded. "One went to the hospital though. I'm not sure yet if she's going to make it." His gut tensed at the thought of Dana Wilson dying. She didn't seem that old, maybe a little younger than himself.

"I've been lucky. Haven't had any deaths yet, but I feel like I'm waiting for the other shoe to drop. Know what I mean?"

Bo rubbed the back of his neck and his hand came away sweaty. "Yeah, I do. Instead of feeling confidant in my ability to save everyone, I feel like I'm waiting for my first fatality. Captain Stewart says you remember every one. I don't want to remember any."

"I hear you." Cole turned his head as a Dallas Fire

Department SUV rolled up. "That must be my boss for the remainder of the night and probably morning." He grimaced.

At least he could be thankful his shift ended soon. "Hey, so have they taught you yet why someone would want to start a fire on the second floor of a three story building?"

Cole turned toward him. "Yes, and it isn't good."

He furrowed his brow. "I didn't expect it would be with arson."

"Right. Sorry, still waking up. They had us in class until nine last night and we had homework."

Bo opened his mouth to ask about that, but Cole shook his head and responded. "The reason the fire in this building was started on the second floor was because someone in that building was the target. Someone on the second floor."

Bo's blood stilled at Cole's statement. Burning a building for insurance money was one thing. Burning it to kill someone was a different matter altogether.

"I've got to go. We're still on for Johnny's Sports Pub tomorrow night, right?"

He nodded before his friend turned and headed for the fire investigator just now exiting his vehicle.

Who was the target of the arsonist? He scanned the buildings' residents, particularly those who resided on the second floor. There was a man about his age with a Chihuahua in his arms, the Sheridans and their cat Misty and Dana Wilson. But there had been four apartments. Was it one of the three here or the mysterious fourth occupant? Was it Dana Wilson?

A chill ran up his back. Had the arsonist succeeded?

~~*~~

Dana opened her eyes, but quickly closed them again. *Crap.* The lowlighting and tan room could only mean one thing. She was in the hospital…again.

She covered her eyes with her hand and slowly opened them. There was a window and the sun streamed into the room. That was nice. She hoped she had a roommate because individual rooms were murder on her budget.

She turned her head and something on her face moved with her. Oxygen mask. *Uh-oh, that wasn't a good sign.* She raised her hand to remove the mask, but before she could, someone grabbed her wrist.

"Hey, you're awake."

She looked toward the feminine voice and found Laura Owens, the owner of Rainbow Acres Refuge. Dana opened her mouth to ask how long she'd been there, but as she tried to speak, her throat constricted and pain worse than the strep she had three years ago, filled her throat. She swallowed in response then wished she hadn't and grabbed at her neck as if that would help.

"Oh honey, don't do that. Don't speak." Laura's worried tone had her loosening her hold.

She looked at Laura, the tears of pain in her eyes

making her friend blurry, but she could tell Laura had her pale brown hair pulled back in the usual ponytail. She pointed to the plastic bubble on her face and at the room.

"You were in a fire at your apartment building. They brought you here to the hospital. You inhaled way too much smoke, so you're on oxygen. They gave you other medicine, too. They called me when they found your phone in your apartment."

Memories of the fire flooded her. Misty! Oh God. Was Misty okay? More tears welled in her eyes, but as her throat closed, the pain returned.

Okay, okay I get it. No crying. But she had to know about Misty. She made the motion of writing with a pen.

Laura's blue gaze lit with understanding. "You want to write something? Okay, hold on." She stood then strode out the door, the unbuttoned long-sleeved shirt she wore over her tank top, the last part of her to disappear.

Please, let Misty be okay. She remembered having Misty tied to her and planned to crawl through the burning doorway, but she lost consciousness. Misty was only a fraction of her size. Poor kitty.

Tears threatened again. *No. Stop. What are you, a masochist? There's no crying after smoke inhalation.* Fine, she'd just think about something else until she could write to Laura. So who rescued her?

It had to be the firefighters. She owed them a big thank you. Maybe they would like a pet from Laura's place.

"Here we are." Laura breezed back in and a nurse

followed her. "She has to see how you're doing then I can give you this." She held up a pad and pen.

With her eyes on the writing instrument, Dana kept herself still as the nurse checked the machines and asked her a couple questions that she nodded or shook her head to.

As soon as the nurse left, she held her hand out for the writing materials.

"Wow, this must be important." Laura handed over the pad and pen.

IS MISTY OKAY? THE SHERIDANS' CAT?

Laura read the message. "Oh, I don't know."

She wrote underneath it. CAN YOU FIND OUT? PLEASE?

Laura's face softened in sympathy. "Of course. The Sheridans are your neighbors, right?"

She nodded.

"They haven't come by to visit, but the other woman on your floor, Tanya, I think her name was, stopped by. She's a little strange. She seemed *relieved* that you were asleep."

Dana nodded. That made sense. She always had the feeling that Tanya really didn't like her, but since she dog-sat for Tanya, her neighbor was civil. Tanya probably came by to be sure her dog sitter was still alive.

"Oh, and a man." Laura frowned for a moment then she smiled. "Jim, that was his name. He stopped in too. He said he was your neighbor."

Jim Lawrence lived on the first floor. She only knew him because they both had a similar schedule and ran into each other often at the mailboxes. He was a nice guy, but a lot older than she was. He was some kind of legal researcher for a big law office.

She was glad Tanya hadn't been home. She must have had her dog with her because a person couldn't walk down the hall without her Maltese barking. With the smoke detectors going off, the dog would have been non-stop and she'd heard no barking.

She refocused on her pad and wrote down the Sheridans' phone number, the word MISTY, then ripped the paper from the pad and handed it to Laura.

Her boss and only friend in Dallas understood. "I'll be right back. You okay if I leave you alone for a few minutes?"

She nodded again.

Once Laura left, she tried not to think of Misty. She rubbed her eyes to keep from crying and focused on what she was supposed to do at the ranch. It wasn't really a ranch. It was more of a house with three additions built on, a couple of kennels and a barn that could hold about two horses. Laura didn't turn any animal away, no matter its condition.

Luckily, the woman was really good at raising money. Dana was supposed to take care of the animals for her as well as meet the volunteer transporters who traveled from neighboring towns to bring them any animal on the list to be put down.

Right now they had a deaf Corgi, a German Shepard with an abscessed foot, a new litter of kittens, three blind ducks, a pig with worms and a dozen baby chicks that needed her attention. The rest of the menagerie Laura could handle as they only needed feeding and watering. The cage cleaning could wait until the weekend.

She stared at her hospital room door. What was taking so long? Probably Mr. Sheridan giving Laura a hard time.

She glanced at her monitors. How bad was it this time? When she was in a barn fire, she'd only had to stay overnight for observation, but that time she'd walked out on her own two feet after guiding the pregnant mare to safety. This time she hadn't done such a great job. *I definitely need to thank the firefighters.*

The door to her room opened and Laura strode in with a smile. "Misty is on the mend. She's on oxygen and resting comfortably at the vet's."

Dana sighed with relief into the oxygen mask. Limbs she didn't know were tense suddenly felt like oatmeal. She'd never come this close to failing a rescue. She wrote on her pad. YAY!

Laura patted her hand. "You did good, kid. Now you need to get well for the others who are counting on you."

She nodded and crossed her chest with her finger.

"You cross your heart you'll do as you're told to get better?"

Dana nodded again and smiled, not that Laura could

really see it. She loved that her boss could read her so well, especially when talking was out of the question.

She'd only worked for Laura a few months, after she had overstayed her welcome in Greenbriar, New Jersey. Shutting down a dog fighting ring had made it too dangerous to stay there. She took risks but she wasn't stupid.

"Good." Laura placed her hand on Dana's wrist. "I need to get back to the refuge and take care of our TLC cases."

She put the pen to paper and wrote. TAMMY NEEDS HER MEDICINE TWICE A DAY.

"Got it."

She turned the pad back and wrote again. DARLING'S BANDAGE SHOULD BE CHANGED AFTER HER DINNER, OTHERWISE SHE GETS IT FULL OF FOOD.

"Okay, I'll do it then." Laura smiled kindly.

She wrote again. BE SURE TO PLACE RANDAL AND—

Laura's hand covered her own, effectively stopping her from writing. "We've got this. You just concentrate on getting better."

She looked up at Laura's smiling face and nodded.

"Good. Now get some rest. I don't need to worry about my star employee with all the animals we have in TLC. When you're better, call me." Her boss walked out the door with that, leaving her alone.

Star employee? I'm your only employee. Dana sighed and let her body relax.

Maybe a few more hours of rest wouldn't kill her. Certainly not like a burning building would. Did they save the building? Did she even have a home left to go to?

~~*~~

Bo moved his large hand up silky long legs that ended in the nicest ass he'd ever touched. His cock hardened. The woman in his arms was sexy and fit him perfectly. Her overly large t-shirt had hiked-up about her waist and he could feel the strands of her long hair where his fingers rested on the small of her back.

Black. Her hair was black.

He racked his brain trying to remember who she was. By the feel of her through her shirt, she was tall and toned, her pert breasts pressed flat against his chest. Had he met her in the gym?

Why couldn't he remember her? There was no way he'd have sex with her if he couldn't remember her name, or where they'd met, or—

She let out a small moan, the sound a pleasant tone.

He had to see her face. Gently, he rolled them over, so she was beneath him. In the darkness of his room he peered at her, but her long hair covered her features. "Hey, are you awake?"

He balanced himself on one arm and pulled her hair away to reveal her face. Her eyes were closed, the long lashes resting against her tanned cheeks. Her nose was slim with a slight upturn at the end and her lips were a deep rose hue, naturally red with no lipstick. As he stared at her, he noticed she wore no makeup at all. He liked that.

Her hair had fallen on his pillow and he could see she had ears that were a bit large for someone with such a narrow face, but they were elegantly shaped as was her neck. Her features jogged his memory but he still couldn't remember her name or where he'd met her. Was it so long ago that it didn't come quickly to mind?

She moaned again or was it a groan and moved beneath him, her skin sliding against his and causing him to grow even harder. He wanted more than anything to wake her up with a kiss, but he couldn't bring himself to do it without a name.

He glanced down at her perfectly shaped breasts, her nipples the color of her lips, but not erect in her sleep. Who was she?

Something soft brushed against his leg and he looked over his shoulder. A furry white cat rubbed its head against his calf, its purr loud in his silent room. At the sight, his brain tripped into gear and he knew who his lover was.

"Fuck."

Bo opened his eyes in shock, relieved to find his black cat Buca sprawled over his feet. It was a dream.

Why had he dreamed about sex with that woman? He swung his legs over the side of his bed and sat staring at the clock. It was just past one in the afternoon. That gave a new meaning to the phrase catnap. He'd only been asleep a couple hours.

Running his hands over his face, he blinked a few times as Buca jumped down and rubbed against his calves, the feeling eerily echoed the one in his dream.

He'd never fantasized about someone he'd rescued before, never mind having them in his bed. It was just weird. When Lexi called and told him they had stabilized the woman and she'd probably be treated and released, he'd finally felt successful.

What Dana Wilson did was irresponsible. She could have been killed. Maybe he dreamed about her because he wanted to let her know the danger she'd put herself in.

Right. So why was he ready to have sex with her while she slept? A dream interpreter would probably say it was him exerting power over her or some stupid nonsense. The fact was, when he'd found her, she was naked from the waist down and despite focusing on getting her out alive, he'd noticed her state of undress. It didn't mean anything more than that, except maybe he was long overdue for a date.

He stood, wide awake now, and stepped around his cat. He'd go back to the apartment building and talk to the Dana woman to avoid any more strange dreams.

They'd let everyone back into the building once it had been inspected for structural stability, except for the two apartments closest to the fire. Those were probably not available, but he doubted there was much left in them anyway.

Since he was off now for a couple of days and had a night out with Cole planned later, he might as well visit Miss Wilson and put a little fear of fire into her.

31

Chapter Three

Having showered, Bo dressed in a pair of jeans, blue t-shirt and cowboy boots. Checking Buca's food dish, he topped it off with a teaspoon of banana ice cream, the cat's favorite monthly treat. "See you tonight, buddy."

Grabbing up his black Stetson, he stepped out onto the porch of his house. He smirked at the cat as he locked the door. Sometimes it was as if he had a dog. Buca sat perched on the back of the couch, watching him from the bay window. He waved and jogged down the three steps to the walkway. He'd left his pick-up outside the garage since he planned to use it later anyway.

The historic section of Dallas with the preserved homes wasn't that far from where he lived. Dana's apartment building was on the outskirts of that. He didn't mind old buildings, but his ten-year-old home was much more to his liking. It was made of the newest fire resistant materials and had hardwired smoke alarms.

Jumping into his truck, he started it up then backed

out onto the quiet suburban street. He didn't need his truck for hauling trailers any more, but once a cowboy, always a cowboy.

It took less than fifteen minutes, traveling the back roads, to get to the site of the fire. To look at the front of the building, the average person wouldn't know there had been a fire.

But he'd helped Tory and Jax break up the couch and throw it out the back hallway window after the Fire Investigator had taken what he needed from it. There were floor boards and wooden slats from the wall on the back lawn as well.

He was surprised to see both the Fire Investigator's and Cole's vehicles were still there. It's not like he was on official fire department business, but it wouldn't be the first time he'd stopped back to see if the people he'd saved were okay.

The stairs were a lot easier to climb without fifty-four pounds of gear on. Before he reached the top, he heard voices. When he stepped into the second floor hallway, he found the Fire Investigator talking to another man while Cole looked on. The back half of the hallway was roped off, a testament to the crime that had been committed.

Cole saw him and walked over. "What are you doing back here already? I thought you'd be asleep, which is where I'd like to be right now."

He looked past his friend at the burnt walls. "Everything okay here?"

Cole shrugged. "Yes and no. The landlord is being very cooperative. It was easy to determine the accelerant used was gasoline and it was poured over that couch your company threw out as well as the walls and floor."

"That sounds promising."

"But we can't tell who the target was. On first glance it would seem to be the couple at that end of the hall or the man who lived across from them."

He nodded. That made sense.

Cole nodded toward apartment 202. "But we can't rule out the single women in each of these apartments because it could simply be that the fire was started at the back because there was something flammable to light. Here by the stairs, there's no furniture, not even a rug."

"I see your point." Bo looked around the landing. There wasn't anything that would feed a fire for any length of time. "But wouldn't the arsonist trail gas toward the apartment he wanted to ignite?"

"Maybe. If the arsonist was a firefighter he would know that these other apartments wouldn't catch before a crew arrived, but if he isn't a firefighter, we can't depend on the criminal having any working knowledge of fires and suppression."

Bo frowned. "But I thought an arsonist is someone fascinated by fire. Wouldn't he know what it did?"

"Normally, I'd say yes, based on what I've learned so far in the classroom, but thanks to this shadowing, I'm getting a crash course on what can trigger an arsonist."

Something in Cole's face had Bo wary. "Why do I get the feeling this is worse than a typical arsonist?"

"Because it is."

Great. Here he was on loan to Station 58 for a month and that's when a killer-arsonist decides to show up. Unless the Fire Investigator could catch this guy right away, the chances of him losing a person to a fire just rose about a hundred percent.

His gut tensed as an image forced its way to the front of his mind of Deacon flailing in the living room of his family's house while fire engulfed his body. Bo shook his head to clear it. "Has the Fire Investigator explained why this is worse than a typical arsonist?"

Cole looked back at the charred floor and doorways for a moment then sighed. "Yes."

The conversation broke up between the Fire Investigator and landlord and both walked toward them. The Fire Investigator jerked his head toward the stairs. "Let's go."

Cole started to follow, but Bo grabbed his arm. He wanted to know what they would be dealing with. "Why is this worse?"

"Because this arsonist has just started to experiment."

Bo let go of Cole as dread spread from his gut to every part of his body. He watched his friend descend the stairs. When Cole disappeared from view, he turned and walked to the rope that cut off the back two apartments and stared at the charred mess. Who do you want? And if you kill him or her, will it be enough?

His entire body chilled at the prospect of the weeks ahead. He'd become a firefighter so he'd never again have to stand helplessly by while another person burned to death. Knowing the chances of that happening again were high, brought back the anger and frustration from his past.

He clenched his fists. Not on his watch. Never again. If he had to—

The closing of a door behind him had him spinning around. He'd forgotten they had allowed the residents back inside since the structure was deemed safe.

"Oh. Who are you?" An attractive black woman in her late twenties with a tiny dog in her arms stared hard at him.

He smiled to put her at ease. "I'm one of the firefighters who worked on the scene this morning."

She looked him over skeptically. "So what are you doing here now?"

His purpose for returning to the building came back with a vengeance. "I'm here to talk to Dana Wilson."

The woman stiffened. "Why?"

"Because…" Actually, it was none of her business. "Because I have information for her about the cat she saved." The lie tripped off his tongue easily.

The woman shook her head. "That cat landed her in the hospital. In fact, that's where you'll find her."

At first he thought the woman was being protective, but now he wasn't so sure. "If your puppy was in your apartment at the time of a fire and you weren't home, would you have wanted her to save him?"

She scowled. "First of all, my dog is full grown, and second of all, *she* is a female. Her name is Tiara." She stroked the white dog in her arms as it lapped her face. She smiled at her pooch before glaring at him. "Lastly, I would never leave Tiara alone at home. She either comes with me or goes to a pet sitter's." The woman glanced at the door across the hall.

Since she'd come out of 202, that meant Dana Wilson lived in 201. That was good to know.

It was clear the woman didn't like him. Not that it mattered. She'd told him what he needed to know. Dana Wilson was still at the hospital.

"Do you have any other business here?" The woman looked pointedly at him. Obviously, he'd overstayed his non-existent welcome. "No, Ma'am." He tipped his hat to her. "Thank you for your help."

As he strode by her, the small dog in her arms looked at him with its mouth open and its tail wagging. Not exactly a protective breed. After opening the front door, he heard her light tread on the steps above him, along with the baby talk she used to communicate with her pet.

He headed for his truck. He'd never talk to Buca like he was a baby. He had a little more respect for his cat than to do that. Once in his truck, he called Lexi to find out which hospital Dana Wilson had been taken to.

In no time he was being ushered into Dana's room. As the door closed behind him, he stared. She slept, her face toward the door and every detail above the oxygen mask was exactly as he'd envisioned it in his dream. His body reacted in a completely inappropriate way, and he gripped the brim of his cowboy hat.

Shit.

Dana opened her eyes to find the man of her dreams staring at her, not that she had a man of her dreams, but if she did, it would definitely be this big, hunky cowboy. She must have done something right in her life to have him in her hospital room.

The man exuded male from his broad, muscular shoulders which were well defined by the tight tee, to his huge biceps, to his square jaw. She'd bet he spent his Sundays playing full tackle football instead of watching it on television.

His brown hair was cut short, but his green eyes were intense, like there was a lot more going on in his brain besides rodeos and beer. His nose and cheek bones softened his look, keeping him from being too hard. But cripes, his body was hard, hard as a Jersey barricade.

She gave him a small smile, not that he could see it. Was he even real? Grabbing her pad that had fallen by her right hip, she quickly wrote. HI.

His brow furrowed. "Hi."

The deep voice with that one word stimulated

parts of her body she hadn't had stimulated by another person in years. Who was he? *Holy moly, let him be in the right room.*

He turned his cowboy hat in his hands. "How are you feeling?"

Crappy. NOT BAD. She showed him the pad.

He looked at it then locked his gaze on her. "It could have been a lot worse."

Huh. How did he know what happened to her? WHO ARE YOU?

"You probably don't remember me. I tried to get you to come out of your burning apartment building, but you ignored me and ran back toward the fire."

Oh, shootin' sheep herders, it was the giant firefighter! If she'd known he was that hot, she would have listened to him.

Hah, who was she kidding? He could have been Prince Charming and she still would have gone back for Misty. She wrote on her pad. SORRY. I HAD TO GET THE CAT.

He shook his head, his frown deepening. "Miss, that wasn't a very smart thing to do. You could have died in there. You need to trust the firefighters to do their job."

Really? He was here to lecture her like she was twelve years old? She was a thirty-year-old woman who was all too aware of what damage fire could do. She pointed to her pad and tapped her pen on the words, I HAD TO GET THE CAT.

"No, you didn't. What you had to do is get yourself

out of the burning building. What if we couldn't contain the fire? You would have died."

She wrote faster. WOULD YOU HAVE GONE IN FOR THE CAT IF I WASN'T STILL IN THERE?

His frown disappeared and his eyes widened. "No, my job is to save people."

Heat rose in her cheeks as her anger surfaced. AND MY JOB IS TO SAVE ANIMALS!

He stared at her pad, puzzlement clear on his face. "Miss Wilson, I don't think you're trained in saving animals from burning buildings. If you were, you—

She wrote furiously as he talked. I AM TRAINED TO RESCUE ANIMALS. I WORK FOR RAINBOW ACRES REFUGE FOR ANIMALS. She spun the pad around, surprised when he stopped talking to read it. *Wow, I'm pretty good if I can interrupt with a pad of paper. Either that or he's too polite to keep talking.*

He looked from the pad to her and back. "If you were trained to rescue animals from a fire, you wouldn't have gone back in."

Was there a training she could take for that? She'd trained in numerous ways from rock climbing, after her scare on the cliff, to safely handling loose electrical wires after her telephone pole episode with the parrot. Now, her curiosity was piqued. She had to ask. WHAT SHOULD I HAVE DONE INSTEAD?

He lost his frown, finally, and she liked him a lot better that way. She was so used to people frowning at her that she had a short fuse with it. Now, he looked like a nice guy. Maybe he could even help her.

"What you should have done was come outside with me and then told me about the cat." He gave her a polite smile.

THEN YOU WOULD HAVE GONE IN?

He moved the cowboy hat in a circle in his hands—his very large hands. "If there was time and I knew about the cat, I would have gone in."

That wasn't what she wanted to know. She wanted to know what she could have done differently given the situation. WHAT IF THERE WASN'T TIME?

He stared at her pad a lot longer than it took to read her words. Finally, he looked at her. "Miss Wilson, you have to understand that I'm trained to save people. Wouldn't you agree that people are more important than animals?"

Of course! She wasn't stupid. That's why she helped the Sheridans. She so wished she had her voice so she could be as condescending as he was. How could she get that across on paper? She swallowed to check her throat and winced.

"I apologize." The cowboy's green eyes softened. "You're still recovering. I will let you rest. Time and rest is what you need. I'm just glad you weren't burned or worse."

He sat his hat on his head and turned away toward her door.

Wait, our conversation isn't over! She scribbled on her pad. WHAT IS YOUR—

He opened the door and looked back at her. "Don't go back into any more burning buildings, please."

"Wai—ack." She grabbed her throat as the door closed. Tears stung her eyes at the pain, but she pushed them back. That would just make it worse. *Cowboy, we are not done here. I'm going to find out who you are and set you straight.*

So much for the man of her dreams. He was like every other man in authority she'd ever encountered. It might be said that a woman had to kiss a lot of frogs before she found her prince, but as far as she was concerned, she'd rather have a frog.

~~*~~

Dana strode out of the Baylord Pet Shelter with a lighter heart. After three days, she was back to work fulltime, doing what she loved. Two dogs and a senior cat would all be going to Rainbow Acres Refuge by this evening. She stopped in every Sunday to discover which animals would be put down on Monday, then came back in the evening right after closing and picked them up.

Luckily, there were very few kill shelters in the city of Dallas. Not like in some of the other places she'd worked. She'd even heard of county commissioners in some states trying to pass legislation regarding how long a pet could stay in a shelter before being euthanized. One nut suggested any dog over six be put down upon entry. Really?

Yup, she was liking the Dallas area more and more. It

seemed to have a good heart for animals. Unlocking her light brown SUV, she jumped in and started it up, setting the air conditioner on high. The temperature had gone far beyond eighty, "a hot one for May" the shelter owner told her, and she'd parked on the street in full sun.

She grabbed up the note she'd thrown on her passenger seat and plugged in the address for Fire Station 58 into her GPS. So many men had talked down to her throughout her career that it was like water off a duck's back by now. But for some reason, hunky cowboy/giant firefighter pissed her off. Maybe because he never finished the conversation with her when she was in the hospital.

Or maybe because he went out of his way to start the conversation in the first place. *That was probably it.*

Pulling out of her parking space, she spent the next twenty minutes navigating the traffic and planning her argument. She could kill two birds with one stone on this visit. She could discover if there was some kind of "putting out fires and rescue" training she could take as a citizen, and set the record straight with Prince Not So Charming.

When she arrived, she parked on a side street and walked up to the open garage door. She could see a couple of men washing one of the engines in the driveway. One had no shirt on and the other's t-shirt was plastered to his body. A definite distraction.

A few men stood off to the side just inside the open bay. Two wore uniforms and the other was dressed in shorts and a t-shirt. The casually dressed man yelled over to the men at the engine. "Rick, you missed a spot."

"Better watch it, Tory, or the minute you step away from the Captain, you're going to get wet."

The casually dressed man, Tory she presumed, grinned. "Maybe, maybe not."

She wasn't dressed up either but she still didn't want to risk getting sprayed, so she made her way closer to the uniformed men. "Excuse me. Could you help me?"

She spoke to the official looking men, but Tory turned around to look at her.

"Oh, better watch out, Tory. Turning your back on us, isn't so smart."

The man called Tory gave the men the finger.

"Don't mind them, Miss. How can we help you?" The distinguished, slightly gray-haired man with a name plate that read Stewart on his breast smiled at her.

"I'm looking for one of your firefighters. He's very tall and broad and wears a cowboy hat."

The other man in uniform with a name badge that read Boone answered. "That's got to be Jax."

"Or Fletch," the Captain added.

"That's right." Boone looked at her. "We have two on this shift, at least for this month."

"Oh." She hadn't counted on that.

Boone continued. "I think Jax is upstairs, but Fletch is washing the truck." He looked past her and yelled. "Hey, Fletch!"

She turned around to see the man of her dreams walk around the back of the engine in nothing but a pair of shorts and sneakers, a soapy sponge in his hand. Suds and water dripped down his chest and onto his shorts. He wore no hat and he squinted as he looked over, but there was no mistaking that body.

"Yeah, Lieutenant?"

"Is that the man you're looking for, Miss?"

She swallowed hard at her suddenly dry mouth and answered. "Yes. It is."

"Come over here, Fletch. You have a visitor."

She whipped back around to address the Lieutenant. "I didn't realize he was busy. I can come back another time."

The older man frowned at her, but the Lieutenant, grinned. "I'm sure he doesn't mind taking a break. Right Fletch?"

She turned around to find "Fletch" just three feet away.

"Dana Wilson?" His eyes rounded and he took a step back. Then he addressed Boone and Stewart. "Captain, Lieutenant, this is Dana Wilson, one of the people we rescued from the apartment building early Thursday morning."

She turned away from the hard abs and muscle-bound shoulders that made up Prince Charming and smiled politely at the uniformed men.

Stewart nodded. "It's very nice of you to show your appreciation, but it's all part of their job."

She kept the smile pasted on her face, not willing to disabuse him of his assumption. But she was happy he reminded her of why she was here. She finally faced her rescuer. Now, she just needed to get "Fletch" to put on a shirt so she could concentrate.

"I didn't expect to see you." His tone made it sound like he was happy she stopped by.

She needed to keep looking at his emerald green eyes and not at what was below them. "I have a few questions for you."

He looked around her. "Mind if I take her inside?"

At the approval of the uniformed men, he ushered her into the shade of the large bay. He stopped by a chair that had a pile of towels on it and quickly dried himself off.

She thought he would take her inside the building but instead, he guided her behind more emergency vehicles to a corner that looked like a mechanic's shop.

Bo still reeled from seeing Dana. Her face was breathtaking and she stood with a bearing that had him intrigued, in a good way. He'd noticed her intelligent hazel eyes at the hospital, but her straight nose and wide mouth with the deepest color lips he'd ever encountered had his body more than paying attention.

Couple that with her extra height and long, wavy black hair, and he was more than mildly interested. He was captivated.

He stopped behind the ambulance his cousin rode in and faced Dana. "You're taller than I expected."

Her eyebrows lowered in puzzlement. "Maybe because I was lying down both times you met me."

The sound of her voice made him think of a day spent in bed making love. "Your voice is husky. Is that normal or is that the residual effects of the smoke?"

She met his gaze, hers having turned almost blue. She cleared her throat. "This is my normal voice."

"I like it." He liked a lot about her. She had an energy that seemed to radiate from her as if standing still for too long would make her bolt. He didn't want her to bolt.

Her gaze wandered over his face and down toward his chest.

He didn't know her at all, but he wanted to. "I'm Bo Fletcher, by the way." He paused. "You really are beautiful."

Taking a deep breath, he stepped closer. He had to kiss her. There were a hundred and one reasons why he shouldn't, but he wanted to more than any of them. Tilting her chin slightly upward, he waited, giving her the opportunity to pull away.

She didn't. Her eyes closed and he lowered his mouth to hers. Her lips were soft and pliant beneath his, just as he expected.

Her hands came up against his chest, sending hot fire from her touch straight to his crotch. He wasn't sure if her intention was to push him away or to feel him.

"Ahem. Fletcher, you have another visitor."

He pulled away fast at the sound of Captain Stewart's voice.

"And when you're done here, I want to see you in my office." The Captain gave him a hard look before stepping to the side to reveal the blonde woman who had accompanied him to the corner of the bay.

Shit. It was Mandy, the woman he met Tuesday night when he'd gone out with Cole. What was she doing here? Had he told her where he worked?

"I was just leaving." Dana spun on her heel and stalked around the front of the ambulance.

Chapter Four

Bo looked at Mandy. "I'll be right back." Racing around the vehicle, he caught up with Dana before she walked into view of the other men. He grasped her arm, gently. "Wait."

She stopped and looked at him in surprise, a hint of embarrassment in her eyes. "What?"

"That, what I did, I mean…you came here looking for me. Did you want something?" He hoped she'd come for his phone number.

She looked confused before she shook her head. "It wasn't important."

She turned away and he stepped in front of her. "It must have been for you to come down here. I'd be happy to help in any way."

She refused to look at him and instead moved around him.

"Wait, how can I find you?" He forced himself not to grab her arm.

She didn't look at him, but spoke over her shoulder. "You know where I live."

He watched her leave the bay. She didn't sashay or strut. Her stride was hard, confident, as if she were comfortable in her own skin. He found that very attractive.

"Bo, is there something you want to tell me?" Mandy slipped her arm in his as she moved in front of him to catch his attention, but her height didn't impede his view of Dana, nor did she soothe his tension when he noticed a couple of the guys watching Dana leave.

The woman in front of him placed her hand on his chest, but hers didn't heat him up like Dana's. He lowered his gaze to her. She was definitely pretty in a cheerleader sort of way. He'd bought her a drink after she initiated a conversation, but he hadn't expected to see her again. "How did you find me?"

She cocked her head to the side. "That was easy. You told me you worked at Station 58. It wasn't hard to look that up and get directions."

He disengaged his arm from hers and took a step back. "I think you heard my Captain wants to see me. Was there something you needed?"

She shrugged. "Just to see you again." Her gaze raked over his naked chest, and he suddenly wished he had his shirt on. "I'm really glad I stopped by."

Bo made himself smile politely. "I'm sorry I have to go, but it was nice to see you again."

She laughed. It was a high pitched sound that made

him think of diamonds. That alone had him backing up. "I better get going."

He was open to finding the right woman to share his home with someday, but he wasn't looking for an "in debt ever after" woman, and from Mandy's painted nails, to her designer suit to her artfully arranged hair, a very different look than when he saw her in the sports pub, *expensive* was written all over her. He'd prefer to steer clear of that.

"What about your number?" She pulled out her cell phone from inside a large purse. "I can punch it in."

He kept backing up. "Sorry, I really have to go." As soon as he was around the ambulance, he strode along the backside of the garage and into the building. He usually wasn't such a coward, but Dana had him completely off balance.

Taking the stairs to the Captain's office two at a time, Bo kept seeing Dana's startled look when the Captain caught them kissing. She hadn't expected the strong physical attraction between them.

He grinned as he thought of their last conversation and opened the door to Captain Stewart's office. Nope, there was nothing in his interaction with Dana at the hospital that would have forewarned him either.

"What are you smiling at, Fletcher?"

He closed the door and moved toward the large desk that had a computer on one side and various piles of paper on the other. "Just a memory, Captain."

His superior frowned. "I don't know what you do

down at Station House 23, but I don't approve of my men dating two women at the same time, nor am I happy when my men date people they rescue from burning buildings. You do know that it could simply be some hero worship going on and not real feelings, right?"

Bo opened his mouth to assure the Captain that nothing like that was happening, but the man held up his hand.

"Yes, I know Jax saved Skye from the hotel fire, but that was different. They grew up together. I'm assuming you have never met this Dana Wilson before the fire at her apartment building, correct?"

"Yes, sir, but—"

"As I expected. That means that whatever she feels for you, after only three days, may not last." The Captain walked over to him and put a hand on his shoulder. "I'm just giving you fair warning, son. You're probably better off with the blonde. Now get back down there and put away the gear. The boys finished washing the truck while you were otherwise occupied."

Bo wanted to tell the Captain he was way off base, but he was only scheduled at Station 58 for three and a half more weeks and then he'd be back with his own crew. Better not to rock the boat.

He let the Captain walk him to the door. "Yes, sir."

"Good man."

Bo stood outside the Captain's office. He'd never even think of dating two women at once, but for it to be assumed he did, rankled. He finally walked away, reaffirming his decision not to make a big deal of it.

As he strode into the bay, the three other men he'd been washing the engine with started giving him a hard time.

"Quite the juggler, huh, Fletch?

"Which one is your real flame? Hey, she's Fletcher's flame."

"Is one for day and one for night?"

"Nah, he has them both at the same time."

He smirked despite himself. He didn't mind ribbing from the guys. He wiggled his brows. "If you need lessons, just ask."

The wet sponge hit him square in the chest. He caught it before it could slide off and onto the ground.

Tory laughed. "Just trying to clean you up a bit."

Bo whipped the sponge at Tory's crotch and the man doubled over.

Grasping the sponge, Tory stood straight again and lifted it away from his khakis. "Shit, I look like I just peed my pants."

Bo shrugged. "Better that than the bed."

The guys behind Tory ooohed, their smiles proving they were loving it. Tory grabbed a bucket of soapy water nearby.

Bo dove for the sprayer and the water fight was on.

~~*~~

Dana finished brushing Cyclone and stepped off the stool. "You're a good looking horse, handsome." She patted his side, letting him know she was done. *But you're not the only one who's handsome. That firefighter has me all hot and bothered now.*

She needed to remember Bo Fletcher's condescending lecture in the hospital and not his muscular chest and commanding lips. How could she have let him kiss her? *I would have had to be made of stone not to let him.*

"Now we just need to find you a new home and a pretty filly. What do you think about that?"

The horse stomped his foot, and she laughed. "I'm glad you agree." *Maybe that's what I need, a date, but not with a man who thinks I'm stupid but pretty enough to kiss.* To be fair, he did like her voice and her height didn't bother him at all. She shook her head. *Nope. Not going there.*

Putting the curry comb away in the cabinet built into the wall of the tiny barn, she shook her head at the horse. "I can't believe no one has adopted you yet. But don't worry, it will happen someday."

Cyclone stomped his foot again and shuffled backward.

"Oh, come on. Sharing your space with a sheep isn't that uncomfortable." She looked over the half wall that divided the structure in two. "Molly's a great roommate. You're going to miss her when she leaves next week."

Cyclone didn't react, having found his dinner.

Just as well. She needed to get back into the city and

pick up their new visitors. She secured his stall with a crowbar between two iron loops. Cyclone would kick the door open if she didn't. Clydesdales were strong.

Closing the barn doors behind her, she headed for the second kennel, waving to the three dogs in the other one who barked excitedly as she strode by. "You guys are all fed and watered. Tomorrow morning Sadie and Betty will be here to play with you."

When she arrived at the second kennel, she took the dog bone she had in her pocket and placed it on the clean doggy bed, all ready for the Collie mix she'd be bringing back. Then she continued into Laura's sprawling house.

Each room was designated by animal and need. The senior cat would stay in Laura's room her first night, but the other dog would be added to the small dog room, *if* he was friendly.

She grabbed a bone from the cabinet in that room and placed it on the bed in a roomy cage then she closed the door. "No, Putsy, you've had plenty to eat already today."

The Schnauzer mix in the next cage cocked his head as if completely baffled by what she said. She chuckled before giving him a quick pat on his nose. "I'm not falling for that, silly pup."

Straightening, she walked into the storage room and retrieved a new knitted blanket. There were still three left, but she'd let Laura know they were running low.

Laura had a wonderful group of volunteers, and some of them made lap throws for the cats. She placed the blanket in a heap at the end of Laura's bed. She hoped the twelve-year-old kitty she brought back would last longer than the last senior cat she saved.

Henry had been fifteen and didn't last more than six months, thanks to cancer, but he had a comfortable and loving final life with Laura.

With everything ready for the new arrivals, Dana stepped into Laura's office. Her boss was on the phone, so she mouthed that she was leaving and grabbed up her keys.

I love my job.

She had that thought at least twenty times a day. She could probably make more money as a teacher now that she had her online Bachelor's degree in education, but it just wouldn't be as fulfilling as what she did now.

As she headed into the city, the traffic slowed to a crawl. Once she and the rest of the thousand cars squeezed around the accident in one lane, she glanced at the clock. *Crapola, I'm late. Mr. Shaunessy better still be there. If not, I'm camping out overnight and I'll wait for him to show in the morning.* No way would she let any animal be put down.

As she pulled onto Renard Drive, red lights reflected off the buildings. The flickering reminded her of her entrance into hell at her own apartment. Another fire? She made the turn onto Pleasant Lane and pulled over.

No! No!

The animal shelter, tucked between a warehouse and a thrift store, was covered in flames. Water from two firehoses sent smoke billowing into the air.

The animals! She ran toward the building, her destination the back door, when something caught her around the waist, knocking the wind from her. When she discovered it was a man's arm, she struggled wildly. "Let me go! There's over twenty animals in there!"

"We know. They're going to be alright."

The familiar voice in her ear caught her by surprise. Turning, she found the man that had kissed her for the first time that very afternoon. "Bo, we have to save them."

"We are."

"How can you say that? Look at that fire and smoke." She tried to peel his arm from around her waist, but it was like the lock-down bar on a rollercoaster.

"Dana, listen to me." He squeezed her a little harder, and she lifted her face to look at him again.

"We have the fire under control. See those yellow flames?"

She looked at the building, the gray smoke smothering it but still a yellow flame would burst through. She nodded, swallowing at the smell and remembering the feel of that smoke in her throat.

"Those yellow flames are weak. It's almost out."

"But what about the smoke? The animals? Misty barely made it and I had her low to the floor."

"Look." He pointed to the alleyway between the shelter and the warehouse. "They're bringing them out."

Even as she focused on the firefighters carrying cages, she heard a couple barks. What would happen to them?

What about the ones she'd come to save? "What will they do with them?" She hated the fear creeping into her voice, but she could easily imagine city officials putting them all down because they had no place to house them.

"They're going to Little Critters who will farm them out to the various no-kill shelters in the greater Dallas area because no one shelter can handle them all."

She turned and looked at him. "I should have been here on time. I was supposed to take two dogs and a cat to Rainbow Acres. They were scheduled to be euthanized tomorrow. Do I need to find them or will they also be given to no-kill shelters?"

Bo frowned. "Is that why you're here? Not because you saw the smoke but because you were supposed to be here earlier?"

"Despite what you think, I'm not a fire engine chaser. I was supposed to be here at seven to pick up three animals."

He pulled his phone out and looked at it, then looked at her. "We need to talk to Lieutenant Boone."

She didn't like the hardness of his voice, but as she watched more animal crates being loaded onto a truck, she worried. Maybe seeing the Lieutenant and asking him directly where the animals were going would tell her if it was true or not.

She didn't trust officials when it came to animals. After she'd convinced the police in Greenbriar to shut down the dog fighting ring, they told her all the pit bulls would be adopted out. It was two weeks later when she accidentally discovered that eleven of the fourteen dogs had been put down.

"Okay, let's go talk to Lieutenant Boone." She expected him to let her go, but he didn't. Instead, he continued to hold her waist and guided her around the firetruck where the Lieutenant stood back from the fire, speaking into his radio.

"Lieutenant Boone?" They waited as the man in question barked another command over the radio.

Finally, he looked at them and scowled. "What is it, Fletcher?"

"I think you need to hear this." Bo turned toward her. "Tell him why you're here."

She moved her gaze from intense green eyes to hazel ones. "I was supposed to be here by seven to pick up three animals that were going to be euthanized, but I understand all the animals are going to no-kill shelters. Is that true?"

The man's scowl deepened. "Of course. That's what we always do in situations like this. It's protocol." He turned toward Fletcher. "Why is this important? I'm trying to get this fire doused."

She looked at Bo as well, not sure what the big deal was.

"Sir, this is Dana Wilson. One of the women who lived in the apartment building we rode to on Thursday. The arson fire?"

"Oh."

"What?" She ignored the Lieutenant's surprise to confront Bo. "What do you mean arson? Someone set our apartment building on fire on purpose?"

Bo rubbed the back of his neck as Dana turned her scared gaze on him, but before he could reassure her, his superior spoke.

"Miss Wilson, would you mind staying here for a while? We'll need you to talk to our Fire Investigator."

She looked about to argue, so Bo squeezed her waist and her gaze flew to him. He nodded at her.

She turned back to Boone. "I don't have to return to Rainbow Acres now, if I'm sure *all* the animals are going to be safe."

Boone nodded, his face relaxing, which made him a lot less intimidating. "I assure you, Miss Wilson, that every single critter will arrive safely at a no-kill shelter after being thoroughly examined by a vet."

She stared hard at the Lieutenant then sighed. "Okay, I'll stay."

Boone moved his gaze to him. "Fletcher, watch out for Miss Wilson while we finish dousing this fire."

"Yes, sir." He guided Dana from the command spot to a relatively quiet area away from the rescue crew and the gawkers that had come out to watch a building burn.

Cole had regaled him the other night with his story about putting out a fire on a nudist resort where his wife worked. He said naked people had driven over in golf carts to watch the fire. Bo couldn't imagine that. He'd bet Cole had exaggerated.

What his friend hadn't exaggerated was that arsonists like to watch the fires they start.

Bo scanned the onlookers. A blonde with a face he remembered caught his attention, but when he looked back, he couldn't find her. What would Mandy be doing at an animal shelter fire? It was probably just someone who looked like her.

He continued to study the crowd. One of the people with their backs to him could be here to see if Dana had died in the fire.

A chill stole through him at that thought, and he walked Dana past the area he'd planned to stop at and took them around the corner where they couldn't see the burning building but he would see the Fire Investigator pull up.

The minute they'd arrived on scene, they'd known it was arson.

"What are you doing, walking me home? I thought your boss wanted me to stay." Dana pulled away from him.

He stopped at her question. "I just want to keep you at a safe distance."

She rolled her eyes. "I think a half mile back that way would be safe. I can't even see the building from here or the animals. Or is that what you wanted me to forget about, the animals?"

He grabbed her by the shoulders to face him, needing

to get her to understand the serious danger she was in. "Listen, sometimes it's about more than the animals."

Her eyes widened. "Of course there's more to it, but you, your boss, the Fire Inspector and even the neighbors are going to be concerned with keeping people safe and stopping the fire from spreading."

His muscles relaxed at her words. He'd been afraid she was one of the militant animal rights people, but she was obviously simply very concerned.

"That's why I have to be focused on the animals. They are a second thought to everyone else, so they need to be my *first* thought. They can't speak up for themselves. That's my job."

He tensed, his relief short-lived. "Dana, this isn't about the animals. This is about arson."

He felt her body freeze beneath his hands, her shoulders stiff. "What do you mean? Wait, you said that someone set my apartment building on fire."

Even in the growing darkness, he could see the fear in her eyes. He wanted to assure her she was safe, but he needed her to understand her own danger. "Yes, the Fire Investigator discovered accelerant had been used on the couch in your hallway before it was torched."

She frowned. "And here?"

He squeezed her shoulders gently, wanting to comfort her, but holding himself back. "We found a deliberate pattern to the fire. It was started intentionally."

She looked away, obviously processing the information.

"I'm not an expert, but in talking to a friend of mine who is being certified as an arson investigator, this arsonist is just getting started."

Her gaze flew back to him and her eyes widened. "I was at both places. Is he targeting me?" Her throat worked as she swallowed hard, but her voice still came out barely above a whisper. "Does he want me dead?"

Chapter Five

Bo couldn't resist any longer, his protective instincts rising up hard. He pulled her against him and wrapped his arms around her. "Don't worry. We aren't going to let that happen."

Her head rested against his shoulder, but her arms remained limp at her sides. She wasn't shaking or crying, two reactions he expected from a woman who had just been told an arsonist was out to kill her.

Curious, he gently pushed her back.

Her brow wrinkled in confusion and her dark lips were pursed together tightly on one side. Finally, she met his gaze. "Do you know who it is?"

He shook his head. "No. So far the only two arson fires we've had this week were your apartment building and this shelter." The rest were accidental or people just being stupid."

He frowned as he remembered the drug addict mom who caught her apartment on fire lighting up crack. If not for her ten-year-old, she and her two kids would have been toast by the time his crew arrived. It had been their first call of his shift.

"I think I know who it might be." Dana's shoulders straightened beneath his hands and her chin came up a notch.

This woman's courage had his heart taking notice, but he kept his mind focused on the problem at hand. "You do? Who?"

"I think it might be one of the men who owned pit bulls in the dog fighting operation I got shut down in Greenbriar, New Jersey. I moved to Dallas after my life was threatened. I thought they wouldn't follow me. I guess I was wrong."

Shit! He wasn't sure if it was bravery or a lack of common sense, but he definitely admired her. "How exactly did you shut down a dog fighting operation?"

She pulled away from him, putting at least twelve feet between them. His gut reacted and he scanned the immediate area, more sure than ever that Dana was the target. The Fire Investigator's car took the turn onto the road with the shelter, but she didn't notice.

"I witnessed the fighting and followed every member to his home, taking pictures of where they lived. I tried to get police to shut it down then, but they said they needed more than just my word and pictures of houses and apartment buildings. So I went back and took videos." She clenched her fists. "It was the hardest thing I've ever done. They pitted the dogs against each other until one was dead."

She stood there, fists clenched with the streetlight reflecting in her tear-filled eyes.

It took all his willpower to stay where he was. "Does that mean you didn't have to testify? Did you take the stand?"

She nodded, but didn't say a word.

Fuck. She was lucky she hadn't been shot. Even the thought of her taking videos secretly had his heart dropping. They needed to tell Boone. Damn, he needed to protect her until they found the bastard that was setting the fires.

It all made sense. Cole said it wasn't a pyro, but a newbie, and what better way to kill Dana and not trace it back to the scum in Greenbriar.

Her mission in life may be to save animals, but now his was to save her. He scanned the area again to make sure no one watched them, but it was empty.

He strode toward her. "Let's go back. The Fire Investigator is going to want to know what you just told me."

"Of course." She didn't look at him. Instead, she turned away and headed back toward the animal shelter.

He didn't let more than a foot separate them as he followed her, watching the onlookers slowly dispersing now that the excitement was over and the smoke had diminished. When they arrived at the command spot, Boone wasn't there, but Cole was.

"Hey, Bo. Looks like you've got another, huh?"

"Yes. Do you know where the Fire Investigator is? Boone wants Dana to talk to him."

Cole's green gaze shifted to Dana. "Are you Dana Wilson?"

"I am."

"Then you are the last person I need to talk to." Cole smiled warmly.

"You?" Bo kicked himself at the sudden spurt of irritation when Dana returned Cole's smile. Cole was a happily married man. He did nothing but sing the praises of his wife, Lacey.

Cole gave him a quizzical look. "Yes, me. The Fire Investigator has me interviewing the witnesses while he goes over the evidence."

Dana spoke up. "Did you say witnesses? Someone saw something?" She gave Bo a worried glance before returning her attention to his friend.

Cole looked down at the pad of paper he held, its small size looked awkward in his large hand. "Yes. There was a Mr. Shaunessy and—"

"That's the owner of the shelter." Dana looked at Cole. "Is he alright?"

"Yes. He just had a little smoke inhalation."

Bo nodded. That made sense. He'd pulled the man out before they even had water on the fire, but unlike Dana, he hadn't been on the floor, instead he stood in his back room coughing. "Who else?"

Cole looked down again. "A Miss Tanya Robinson."

"Tanya?" Dana looked at Bo then back at Cole. "She lives across the hall from me. I dog-sit for her on occasion. What was she doing here?"

"According to my interview with her, she was looking to adopt a pet for her niece, but Mr. Shaunessy wouldn't let her because he was closed. He closed the blinds on her and she pounded on the door yelling for him to open up. I guess she yelled for quite a while with no luck and was about to leave when she smelled the smoke. She walked down the alley toward the back and saw flames, so she called 911."

"That's weird." Dana's frown told him it was more than just Tanya's behavior.

"Why is it weird?"

She looked him in the eye. "Tanya doesn't have a niece."

Cole raised an eyebrow at that information. "She's obviously hiding something. She's also another link between the two fires."

Bo voiced what he'd bet they were all thinking. "She could be the arsonist or the one the arsonist was after and he just didn't know that she wasn't home Thursday night."

"Which brings me to Miss Wilson." Cole focused on Dana again. "Why am I supposed to talk to you? Were you here when the fire started?"

She shook her head and took a step closer to him. Bo put his arm around her shoulders, an action Cole noticed if his look was any indication. "Go ahead, Dana. Tell him about why you were supposed to be here."

While she filled Cole in on her animal pick-up and the dog-fighting ring, Bo watched her carefully. If he hadn't noticed her running toward the building and caught her, she would be considered a suspect.

She was driven beyond common sense. Ordinary people didn't run *into* burning buildings to save pets, which meant she was extra-ordinary. At first he'd been angry she'd risked her life and made his job harder when he had to rescue her from her apartment building.

Then he'd written her off as simply too kind-hearted for her own good when he'd seen her lying in the hospital bed.

It wasn't until she'd walked into Station House 58 that he'd seen her as a beautiful, confident woman, except for perhaps in his dream, but now, after seeing her race toward yet another burning building, he wanted to know what made her tick.

He also wanted to keep her safe.

"So can I leave now?"

Dana's question sent his adrenaline racing. Not by herself she couldn't. "Let me just tell the Lieutenant and I'll escort you home."

Dana's surprised look was mirrored by Cole.

"What?" He addressed Cole. "We just figured out that Dana might be the target of an arsonist. I think someone needs to be sure she makes it home safe."

"I'm perfectly capable of getting in my car and driving myself home *if* that's where I want to go. As a matter of fact, I need to grab dinner first." Dana crossed her arms as if that settled everything.

There was no way he would let her drive across town by herself when the possibility existed that—

"Miss Wilson, I have to agree with Bo."

He snapped his gaze to Cole's. He hadn't expected support from that quarter.

"If the Lieutenant will allow it, I suggest that Bo go with you."

Dana opened her mouth to speak, but Cole held up his hand. "Please. I do feel your life is in danger and if not Bo then I will have to suggest police protection."

Bo started to shake his head, but at Cole's look, he caught on. They both knew the Dallas PD wouldn't assign an officer to Dana. In Texas it was Rangers who provided protection, but for some reason, Cole was helping him out, and he wasn't about to look a gift horse in the mouth. "Listen, Dana. I promise to simply shadow you. I won't interfere at all."

She scowled, obviously not happy with her choices.

He held out his arms. "Come on, I'm not that bad, am I?"

Her lips quirked just a bit. "Will you teach me how to handle myself in a fire? That's why I came to the fire station today. I want to be trained in fire suppression or whatever it is you train in."

Huh? There was no such training unless a person became a firefighter, but she'd get pissed if he told her that. Shit. "I can definitely teach you a few things that could aid you in a fire, *if* you are ever in another one." Now that he'd said it, it made a lot of sense to make sure she knew the basics with an arsonist on her heels.

She stared hard at him in the flickering lights of the emergency vehicles. If he didn't know better, she was trying to decide if he told her the truth. Now that rankled.

She held out her hand. "Okay, you have a deal."

She wanted to shake on it? If it wasn't such a serious situation, he'd laugh with disbelief, but she was completely serious. He shook her hand, surprised how cool it was. The sun may have gone down, but it was still well over eighty degrees even without the remaining heat radiating off the building.

"I'll call Laura." Dana held up her phone. "She's expecting three more animals that won't be coming. Then I'm ready to get out of here."

"I'll talk to the Lieutenant and meet you at your car."

She nodded even as she walked a few yards away to make her call.

Bo turned back to Cole. "Thanks."

"If it was just your interest in her as a date, I wouldn't have said that. But my instructor is confident that this arsonist is going to escalate and if either she or her neighbor is the target, there's a good chance he will succeed unless we catch him first."

"Keep me updated even if it's 'unofficial' information. I want to be one step ahead of this bastard." Bo unzipped his turnout gear, ready to leave the scene as quickly as possible.

Cole stopped him by grabbing his arm. "Hey, what is it with you and this woman?"

He lifted his hand to rub the back of his neck, and Cole let go. "I don't know. She's interesting, in a good way. For now, I just want her to live. That would go a long way in helping me get to know her."

"Okay. Just be careful. I'd hate to see you get burned both figuratively and literally."

Bo chuckled and stepped out of his bunker gear. "Don't worry, I've been through my share of relationships and fires, and I'd say the first is a lot more dangerous."

Cole laughed then headed back toward the street where the Fire Inspector stood next to his SUV, talking on the phone.

~~*~~

Dana finished her second slice of pizza and broke their silent dinner. "You can have the rest."

Bo's large hand stilled on its way to the pizza box. "The rest? You can't be full yet."

She waved him off. "I'm a grazer. I eat a little all day. Go ahead." At his doubtful expression, she nodded emphatically. "If you don't finish it, I'll just bring it to Darling."

He finally picked up another slice which he dropped on his paper plate. "Darling who?" He took a bite of his pizza.

She frowned at him. "Darling the pig at Rainbow Acres. She loves scraps."

At his self-deprecating chuckle, she smiled. "You're not jealous of a pig, are you?"

He finished chewing before he answered. "That depends on if you're talking about an animal or a police officer."

She laughed, which made her feel a little more at ease. Having a man in her new apartment was a first, but having such a large man in it made it feel small, like they were forced to be closer than they needed to be. "I'll take an animal over a cop any day."

"Why?" He looked at her quizzically. "I noticed you don't really care for authority."

She shrugged as she rose and threw out her dirty plate. "Let's just say they've let me down too many times." She leaned her hip against the kitchen counter. She preferred being a little taller than him and it could only happen with him sitting down and her standing.

They'd stopped at the fire station so he could stow his gear and put on his cowboy boots and hat. He'd taken the hat off as soon as they entered the apartment and set it on her vestibule table. At least that table was good for something.

They'd also picked up a pizza on the way, which she

could tell he was enjoying immensely. "What about you? Did you always want to be a fireman when you were growing up, or had you planned to be a rodeo champion and didn't quite make it?"

A fleeting glimpse of pain in his eyes was the only sign that her question had struck a nerve, but he smirked, easily covering it up. If he was that practiced about it, it had to be an old agony.

"Like any tyke, I started out dreaming of the big rodeo buckles, but when I was a teenager I saw a fire and decided I wanted to be less self-involved and help people. Even though I did do the rodeo circuit for a little while during high school. Yes, I won a buckle. But after both Cole and I got busted up riding Hades, I stopped. As soon as I graduated, I went to college for a Fire Science degree and directly into training. I've never looked back. Never lost a person either."

He took another bite of his pizza, which consisted of half the slice, giving her time to digest all that. They weren't really that different when it came down to it. They were both rescuers.

"By the way, it's 'firefighter' not 'fireman.' A fireman is the man that shovels coal into steam engines."

The way he stated it, she could tell he'd done so thousands of times. "I'll remember that." He would be a good one for talking to kids in the classroom. His friendly smile, polite manners and overall large presence would have both boys and girls worshipping him as their hero.

She crossed her arms over her chest. In reality, he was *her* hero. He saved her from her own burning building. She was also impressed with his size and the muscles beneath his t-shirt and pants. So why couldn't she relax around him?

Because he's one of those male authorities I can't trust. Just like dad, pretending to be important, when he was passed over for promotion. Telling her mom he had to work late and then coming home smelling like pot roast. Not that he'd let her mom spend money on a roast.

"Your turn. How did you get into rescuing animals? Last I heard, there was no school you can go to in order to be trained in that." Though Bo smiled as he asked, her defenses went up.

"Actually, those who work in animal welfare in certain cities get extensive training, and there is wildlife management training as well. I did take a few of those, but for the most part, it's all on-the-job training. Sometimes off the job, too."

He picked up the last piece of pizza. "What type of job?"

She shrugged, starting to relax. "I've only worked for nonprofits that save animals. It's the best way for me to help because there is never enough staff so as an employee, I get to do everything eventually." Usually she'd stop her explanation with that, but Bo didn't appear bored. He focused all his attention on her, even missing the fact he had a bit of tomato sauce on the side of his mouth.

"I've always worked for rescues and shelters that don't

put down animals. If I'm going to put my life in danger to save an animal, I certainly don't want it killed just because it hasn't been adopted in a certain amount of time."

"That makes a lot of sense."

"I also focus on domesticated animals, not wildlife, though I have rescued a few of those when they have been endangered by humans."

At his look of curiosity, she dropped her arms and explained. "For example, I was driving on the Kancamagus Highway in New Hampshire when the pick-up truck in front of me hit a white-tailed deer. The driver stopped and called the wildlife department to let them know and waited for them to arrive. What he didn't realize was that when he hit the adult, her body slammed into her baby, who fell over the side of the road. So I went down and rescued it."

Bo put down his half eaten piece of pizza. "Rescued it from what?"

"Down the side of the road was a bit of a cliff and the fawn had tumbled down to a shelf. It bleated for its mother, but otherwise was unhurt. It tried to scamper back up, but fell again, and I could see it could easily go over the edge, so I climbed down to make sure that didn't happen."

"And you climbed up with the fawn?" Bo's doubt was obvious.

"Of course not. It was a cliff. I kept the fawn on the ledge until the wildlife management rescued us. After that, I took a few lessons in rock climbing, in case I found myself in a similar situation."

Bo nodded. "Which is why you want to learn about being safe in escaping a fire."

"Yes." That he understood had her pulse racing. "The more I learn, the better prepared I am and the less danger the animal and I will be in next time."

Bo finally took his gaze off her and brought the last part of the pizza to his mouth.

She watched as he folded up his paper plate and with a stretch of his arm, dropped it in her trash basket. That arm bulged with muscle, causing his department t-shirt sleeve to stretch to the maximum. No wonder he rescued people. He had the sheer strength to do it.

He stood, causing her to switch her gaze to the rest of him. She was tall for a woman at six feet one inch, but he had to be at least six six. For an authority type, he actually seemed like a decent man. She had been enjoying his company and now he'd have to leave. Her disappointment surprised her.

It must be the cowboy side of him she related to. He, at least, understood animals. Reaching behind her, she picked up her keys. "You left your vehicle at the fire station, right?" She could ponder her interest in him after he was gone.

Bo didn't move toward her vestibule to pick up his hat. Instead, he crossed his arms and shook his head. It was an intimidating look. She hated that look.

"Dana, I'm not going anywhere."

Chapter Six

A tiny slice of panic started in Dana's belly. "What? You have to. You have to go home and go to work."

"I don't think you understand. You have an arsonist on your tail, and I'm here to protect you. I don't work again for two more days, so I'm sticking close. Tomorrow when you have time in your schedule, we can stop at my place so I can pick up a change of clothes. My guess is you don't have anything here that I could wear." He winked, which spoiled his intimidation look, but sent another whole vibe through her body.

She swallowed hard. This wasn't what she'd expected when she'd agreed to let him come home with her. "I thought…"

Bo moved around the table to stand in front of her. "I know this is hard, but it's only for a short time. Just until they can find this maniac."

Her stomach felt like it was in her throat. "What if they never find him?"

"Then I guess I'll have to stay with you forever." He grinned.

Her face must have reflected her panic because he raised his hands in surrender. "No, I'm kidding. They'll find him. Don't worry."

She slid her hips along the counter until she could walk out from behind the table and into her living room. "I think you're making more out of this than there is. It could be Tanya that is the target or it could simply be coincidence."

His eyes reflected hurt before he scowled at her. "If not me, then the police."

"No!" She'd never trust an officer again. Her father had lied to her and her mother too many times to count, finally shacking up with her mom's cousin and blaming her mom for that, too. "I mean, if that's my only choice, then I'd rather have you as my watch dog."

"Why do I get the feeling you're choosing the lesser of two evils?"

"It's not personal. I just don't know you."

Bo rolled his eyes and repeated. "I saved you from a burning building while you were unconscious and half naked. I think you can trust me."

Her pulse slowed at that. He made a good point. Maybe she could trust him not to take advantage of her, but could she trust herself not to take advantage of him? The kiss in the fire station brought her body back to life and she wasn't immune to the memory of him holding her at the fire tonight.

He was hard, strong, easy to rely on. That in itself scared her. She didn't rely on people like him. She pointed to the couch. "I don't have another bedroom. All I have is this couch and it's not even a pull out."

"Not a problem." He strode over and sat on it as if testing it. He leaned back, stretching out his long legs and crossing them at the ankle. "Perfect."

She had to smile. "Really? That thing has to be two feet too short for you."

"Hey, beggars can't be choosers."

Should she offer him her bed? She really didn't want him to stay, so if he insisted then he could suffer with it. *But he's staying to protect me.*

She pushed her thought away. "Let me see what I have for extra sheets and blankets." Walking into her bedroom, she let out a breath.

There hadn't been a man in her house since she was eight years old. She'd had a few relationships, but had always managed to go to her "boyfriend's" house. Of course, none of them lasted. They all wanted too much of her time and didn't understand the risks she took for animals.

She moved to the closet and pulled her extra set of sheets for her bed from the top shelf. At least they were king sized, though she wondered if he would even fit on a bed that big. She didn't have any extra blankets, but there was an afghan on the chair he could use.

She glanced at her bed and paused. She really should offer it to him. He'd probably say no, since he was raised that way, but the chip on her heart just wouldn't budge, and she finally gave up.

He would need a pillow because she didn't have the fancy couch pillows other people had. She grabbed one from her bed and headed back toward the living room.

When she entered, she found him holding the picture of her receiving the Citizen of the Year award in Gasten, Mississippi.

"I see you were honored."

She shrugged, a little embarrassed he'd seen it. "Here's a set of sheets and a pillow." She stripped the pillow of its case. "And if you need a little warmth, there's this afghan." She dumped the pile on the easy chair.

He held up the photo. "Citizen of the Year?"

He wasn't going to let it go, was he? "You want to know why I got it, don't you?"

Bo grinned, his green eyes lighting up like a young boy who'd just been told he could have ice cream for dinner.

She sighed. "I just did my job. I saved some animals when the town flooded. It's a small town and most of the people there were very attached to their pets."

She moved into the kitchen to grab a bottle of water for her bedside. "A lot of people lost their homes and the shelters wouldn't take pets, of course. Those places are chaos with humans, never mind throwing pets into the mix. So I opened my house for all the animals and took care of them with volunteers until people could take their pets back."

She closed the fridge and looked at him. "Do you know that every single owner came to visit their pet once a day, except those who were hospitalized. I was able to recruit volunteers to bring those people their animals a couple times a week."

"That's impressive." He put the picture down. "I'm guessing you went into the flood waters to retrieve the animals."

Crap. Now he's going to lecture me on letting rescue crews do their jobs.

He opened his mouth, but she didn't let him speak. "Luckily, I was able to obtain a canoe. All the other boats, and there weren't many, were being used by emergency personnel. I got to one dog just in time. He was on a chain bolted to the cement patio trying to keep his head above the rising water. I took his collar off and dragged him into the canoe. He was so tired he just lay there shivering. I covered him with my coat until I could get him to dry land and my crew of volunteers."

He didn't respond, but he did close his mouth.

"Anyway, I have to get up at five tomorrow. Do you plan to go everywhere I do?"

He nodded but still didn't say anything.

"Okay, well, goodnight." She turned toward her bedroom but hadn't taken one step before his voice stopped her.

"Why animals?" His tone was gently curious.

However, his question caused a maelstrom of

emotions to swirl within her. Images of her childhood stray cat, her father, the argument, the pain. She choked down the lump in her throat and blinked at the tears. *I am not going there.* Without turning around, she threw her answer over her shoulder. "Why not?" Her voice, far raspier than usual, wasn't very loud.

When his step sounded on the wood floor behind her, she jumped into motion, quickly striding out of the room to her bedroom where she closed the door.

Crapola, there's no lock. Not one of the modern conveniences the landlord had thought to add to a one-bedroom apartment in a hundred-year-old building.

She leaned her back against the door and listened for his footsteps. She heard them, but they didn't come any closer. He was probably making his bed. Finally pushing away, she placed the water bottle on her nightstand and changed into her extra-large t-shirt. The water was a new habit she'd started after the fire. She woke up a few nights with a sore throat and the water helped.

Ready to brush her teeth, her hand was on her doorknob when she stopped. She hadn't told him where the bathroom was.

Listening through the old six panel door, she heard nothing. Stealthily, she opened it an inch and peered across the way to see her bathroom door shut. *Yup, he found it.* She closed the door and sat on the bed, listening for him to leave.

Maybe she should put a chair or something under her

doorknob. Better yet, jingle bells so she would wake if he came in. *Jingle bells? Really? He saved my life. I don't have to worry with him. He's a firefighter, not a cop. He's just a cowboy doing whatever it is they do.*

She'd only met a couple cowboys since she rarely rescued horses, but the few she'd met had been very polite, but distant.

At the sound of her bathroom door opening, she stood. This one wasn't distant. He was very close. He also seemed very personal.

His focused attention on her, what she said and felt, unnerved her. And just gazing at him anywhere below the neck was distracting. There was way too much strength in the man's body for her to be completely immune to the physical attraction sizzling between them.

Plus, she wasn't used to sharing her space with another person. On one hand, she didn't want him in her apartment, but on the other hand, she was grateful and wanted him to feel comfortable.

Wait a minute. Do I still have that robe I bought when I went on the weekend cruise to Cancun?

She walked to her closet and dug through it. "Hah." Grasping the typical white robe with the cruise line name embroidered on it, she pulled it out. It was a "one size fits all" type of thing, so it might just work, though she couldn't imagine the company that made the robe had men the size of Bo in mind.

Pleased she might be able to make him a little more

comfortable, she left her room and walked into the living area. She stopped short at the sight of Bo, butt naked, placing the pillow at the end of the couch.

He stood, and she stopped breathing.

Every inch of the man was solid muscle from his ripped abdominals to his corded thighs to his bulging calves. She didn't miss the large cock nestled against dark pubic hair either before he covered it with the pillow he grabbed up.

Her whole body heated at being caught staring. "I'm sorry. I didn't know you were, ah, I just thought you might, um—here." She thrust the robe toward him.

He moved forward, the sliver of a smile on his lips. "Thanks, I obviously need it."

Her cheeks heated more at what he must have perceived as an insult. "No, not at all. You have an amazing body. I didn't know you would walk around naked, that's all. I thought you'd be stuck in your jeans so I wanted you to have that." Her voice trailed off as his grin grew wider.

"Thank you."

He didn't move to put it on. He just stood there smiling at her.

She found herself wishing he would drop the pillow and the robe. Holy moly, what had gotten into her?

"So you think I have an amazing body?" His smile had changed, his whole look turning seductive.

Uh-oh, now you're in for it. "Are you fishing for a compliment?"

He took a step forward. "Maybe."

Two could play this game. "If you want one, you'll have to show me everything." She smirked, confident, based on how quickly he'd covered himself, that he would back down.

To her horror and delight, he threw the pillow on the couch and spread his arms. She sucked in a breath as her gaze roamed over every inch of tautness, his cock now hard and protruding outward. When her eyes reached his, he cocked an eyebrow.

Her body revved like an engine ready for the starting gun. Though she should feel embarrassed, she didn't. Powerful was more the feeling, though from the man before her, she should feel weaker than a day-old kitten. She lifted her hand and made a circle with her finger. "Turn around. I need to see everything if I'm going to pass judgement."

She saw more than heard his silent chuckle as he turned his back on her.

Shootin' sheepherders! He was just as hot and tight in the ass as he was in the front. His back muscles rippled as he looked over his shoulder.

"Well?"

She swallowed hard, her belly doing flip-flops over the view of him. "You'll do."

He turned back around and closed the distance in one stride. "I'll do?"

She forced her gaze up to meet his. "Yes." She tried to

grin, to lighten the mood, but the electrical attraction she felt wasn't going anywhere.

"I'll do for what?" He eyed her seriously, all traces of humor gone.

Good question. She didn't have the answer. She couldn't think with him so close, except about how much she wanted to touch his hard chest.

"I don't know. I better go to bed." She started to turn but his hand came down on her shoulder.

It wasn't hurtful, just detaining, holding her there. "Dana." His tone softened and her heart squeezed, a long buried need to be cared for rising up, yelling at her that this man could do it.

She stared at him, her hope fighting with her doubt. Why would he want to care for her? Her own parents fought over who would get custody, neither wanting her. Just because he was strong and caring didn't mean he'd want her either.

His other hand cupped her cheek. "I like you. I find you fascinating, in a good way. Let me kiss you again."

It was no more than a physical want, but at that moment, with all that was happening to her, she'd take it. She gave him the slightest nod possible, but she could sense his tension ease, even as he lowered his head and his lips touched hers.

Like at the fire station earlier, he was gentle, as if she were the most precious person in the world. Her cynical self crumbled as his tongue breeched her lips and explored her mouth. He tasted of mint, and he smelled so masculine, a combination of smoke and musk.

She leaned toward him and placed her hands on his chest. The second she felt his warmth, her nipples hardened. Unable to resist, she smoothed her palms over the mounds of his pectorals, even as she sucked his tongue into her mouth.

His hands left her face and shoulder to pull her tight against him, his strength exciting her, telling her she was safe, cared for, and very much wanted. His mouth became more demanding as his tongue swept over hers and learned every inch of her.

She moaned, pressing her hips against his thighs, her sheath moistening with need. *I want this. Just for tonight. Just to pretend.*

As if he sensed her capitulation, his hand moved to her thigh, stroking upward to her ass where he squeezed one cheek. His own hips pressed his hard cock into her abdomen, setting aflame the tindered ash of her desire. Her sheath contracted.

Bo's hand continued its ascent up her back until he broke their kiss to pull her t-shirt over her head.

As the coolness of the air conditioner touched her skin, her brain started to focus. *What am I doing?*

Before she could react, he was kissing her neck, bending her backwards, trailing nips along her skin until he reached her nipple. His tongue swirled the hard nub then his lips closed over her areola and he sucked.

The tension between her thighs grew, and moisture dampened her outer lips. She wanted him inside her. As his tongue traced a path to her other nipple, she moaned again, finally rasping out what she could. "I need…"

His mouth sucking her nipple hard made her gasp as fire shot from there straight to her core. Then his other hand found her thigh and moved toward her mons.

Oh yes, please. She spread her legs, barely aware he held her whole weight on one arm.

A knock at her door halted everything. "Hey Dana, are you awake?"

Tanya's strident voice impinged on her euphoria, breaking whatever connection she'd let herself make.

Bo must have felt it too. His mouth left her breast as he pulled his hand away and he raised her straight.

She opened her mouth to answer her neighbor, but Bo's shaking head stopped her.

"Dana? Shit. Come on Tiara. I guess you'll have to come with me tonight." Tanya's high-heeled footsteps sounded loud in the uncomfortable silence. *Crap, how did I not hear those?*

Bo still held her, but she stepped out of his embrace and grabbed her t-shirt. Throwing it over her head, she struggled to get her arms in her sleeves, but finally did. She looked at Bo, who watched her, no expression on his face.

"I… I…" What could she say? That is was a mistake? That she wanted him to be her Prince Charming, but that was just a fantasy? She finally gave up saying anything and walked out of the room, her body urging her to go back, her heart begging her to return and her mind telling her to stay as far away from the man as possible.

Bo watched as a myriad of emotions crossed Dana's face, everything from disappointment to hope to fear. But he knew she wouldn't stay. Something in her actions and words over the day told him she wouldn't find fulfillment in his arms after they were interrupted.

He rubbed the back of his neck and sat on the couch, pulling the pillow out from behind him. His body was more than ready for her, but he forced himself to think of something other than her body, Dana as a person instead.

She had more depth than most of the women he'd dated. She had enough layers to keep him digging for years. He'd learned a lot about her in just one day, more from what she didn't say than what she said.

Even as he'd thought of ignoring the uncomfortable moment when she found him naked, there had been such hopeful yearning in her eyes that he'd couldn't resist. It was the same at the station house. She not only attracted him, but she intrigued him.

Lying back, his legs hitting the arm of the couch at his knees, he stared at the ceiling. There was a smoky smell to the furniture thanks to the fire, but not too strong. It actually made him feel at home.

His gut told him the key to unlocking Dana was in her

mission to help animals. If he could discover that, he had a feeling everything would fall into place. The problem was, he was as interested in unlocking her body as her mind and that was a heady distraction.

He put his hands beneath his head. Tomorrow would be enlightening, a day in the life of Dana Wilson. Maybe it would shed some light on what made her tick…and hopefully Cole could shed light on the arsonist.

Bo closed his eyes. Between the short couch and his hard on, he doubted he'd sleep much, but he had no doubt his dreams would be filled with Dana. A very naked Dana. He grinned.

~~*~~

Bo found Dana's life a lot more interesting than his own. He hadn't realized how much time he spent with his firehouse friends. Dana, on the other hand, was around all kinds of people…and animals.

Their first stop that morning had been Rainbow Acres, where she decided he might as well help her with the morning feeding and crap dumping. While comfortable with the cats, dogs, pig, sheep and horse, feeding the bearded dragon, the parrot and the corn snake was a new experience.

Then they were off to the community center where she gave an orientation to prospective volunteers for Rainbow Acres. Their next stop had been a meeting with a woman who gave the term "Cat Lady" a whole new meaning.

Dana hadn't said a word about what almost happened between them last night and he wouldn't bring it up. He'd been ready to continue what they'd started, and his dreams had confirmed that, but he held back. She wasn't ready.

Now they were headed to his house, and while he'd learned a lot about her, he still didn't know what he wanted to know.

He directed her around the last corner onto his street and they pulled into his driveway.

"You live here?"

"Yes. Why? Were you expecting a mansion?" Did she originally come from money? Was that why she didn't trust him?

She snapped her head around to look at him. "No, of course not. I was expecting a ranch."

With his ego soothed, he was able to smile. "I'd love a ranch, but it's a long drive into the city. I know of a few firefighters who own ranches, but they have help. Firefighting and ranching are both full time jobs."

"Then why do you wear cowboy boots and a hat?"

He raised his eyebrows. "You haven't lived in Texas long, have you?"

She shook her head.

"I grew up on a ranch, even participated in the rodeo circuit for a while like I told you last night, but I was meant to be a firefighter. That doesn't exclude me from being a cowboy though. A cowboy is more than just riding horses and roping cattle. It's a life choice, but it's also a way of life, a way to live life." He took a deep breath. "I'm probably not explaining it right."

Her hand on his thigh surprised him.

"No, you explained it perfectly. I get it now."

Her smile was kind. It was the same one she used when talking to the animals. In a way he was insulted, but considering what high esteem she had for animals, he took it as a compliment.

"Come on in." He opened his door and jumped out.

Dana followed him up the small brick path.

A weird excitement built inside him, curious to know what she'd think of his home. After unlocking the door, he pushed it open and stepped back. "Here we are."

Curiosity made her eyes light as she stepped into the small but tall vestibule. Buca waited for them and rubbed against her ankles.

"You have a cat?"

Her surprised tone of voice coupled with the fact that she immediately crouched down to pet Buca had his pride in his home deflating quickly.

Buca, the traitor, was practically in her lap. No, make that now in her arms as she rose with his cat butting its head against her chin.

He closed the front door with a thud. "Yes, I have a cat. His name is Buca."

"Hey, Buca. Did you miss your daddy? He's been

gone a long time, hasn't he?" She gave him a scowl before returning her attention to his cat.

He should have known. Throwing his keys down on the side table beneath an antique framed mirror, he faced her. "Buca is used to my schedule. Twenty-four hours on, forty-eight off. As you can see, it's not as if he missed *me*. He's a rather independent cat."

She cuddled the traitor, scratching behind the cat's ears, causing a purr so loud it almost echoed. "Where did the name Buca come from?"

He headed for the kitchen. "He's black like licorice but I didn't want to call him that." He heard her footsteps following him as her sneakers squeaked against the title. "So I named him after the licorice flavored liquor Sambuca, but as you can see, he's a small cat."

"So you shortened his name." She kicked out a chair in his breakfast nook and sat, the cat still loving all over her.

Damn, to be that cat right now. "It was better than calling him Bananas. He has a freakish love for that fruit." He shook his head.

"I had a black cat once." The soft tone of her voice caught his attention.

"When you were young?" He leaned his butt against the center island in his kitchen and watched her carefully.

She didn't look at him, just nodded, keeping her focus on his cat.

"What happened to him?"

She continued to stroke Buca, who settled down on her lap and lifted his head to receive each new pet.

Just when he thought she would ignore his question, she spoke. "He was poisoned on Halloween. Probably some teenagers did it. You know, all that superstition about black cats. When he came by my house, I wanted to get him to a vet, but I was only eight and my mom didn't want to spend money on a stray."

She paused and he held his breath, not wanting to interrupt, but anxious to learn more.

"Zorro may have started out a stray, but I fed him regularly and hid a cleaned out cottage cheese container full of water behind our shed. He was my cat and he loved me. He was my best friend." The lost expression on her face had him aching for her.

She shook her head. "I threw a temper tantrum, demanding that Mom take him to the vet. By time my dad got home, she was ready to get Zorro help just to shut me up."

His gut twisted. Instinct told him this didn't end well. His own voice was barely above a whisper. "The vet couldn't save him?"

She stopped petting Buca. "He never made it to the vet. My father was pissed at my mom for wanting to spend money on the cat and even angrier at me for being a 'wimp.' He said he'd take care of the cat."

Dana finally looked at him and the agonized grief

in her eyes made him tense. He wanted to know what happened, but her face told him he didn't.

"My dad went out back where Zorro was lying on an old t-shirt of mine, too weak to move and trying to breathe. Dad took his nine millimeter out of his holster and shot him."

Chapter Seven

Stunned, Bo's gut felt like he'd been punched, hard. His heart ached for Dana, an image of her as a child standing in her backyard, tears streaming down her face froze him in place.

She returned her attention to Buca. "Zorro was short-haired like your kitty. Did you know that female all-black cats are very, very rare, but males are common?"

He blinked at her statement. She acted as if she didn't just knock the air out of him with her story. He couldn't stay away from her a moment longer.

It might be an old grief, but he wanted to comfort her. Somehow saying "I'm sorry about your cat" just wasn't enough.

He walked toward her, not sure what he could do, but wanting to offer comfort. Before he reached her, Buca jumped off her lap and rubbed himself across his shins. He lost his balance, and not wanting to step on his cat, he swung his arms wide to catch himself as he hopped over Buca.

He ended up on his knees in the middle of his kitchen floor.

Dana knelt in front of him in a heartbeat. "Are you okay?" Concern mixed with laughter in her eyes.

He smirked, happy to see the sadness gone from her face. "Yes. It's not the first time he's done that."

She smiled that warm smile that wasn't meant for an animal. "I'm sure he has, and yet you and he have both lived to talk about it."

A quip was on the tip of his tongue about how Buca talked enough as it was, but her expression was so unguarded for a change, he couldn't resist. He pulled her to him and kissed her.

Her arms wrapped around his neck and his whole body relaxed with her acceptance. As their tongues entwined, a new need grew, not between his legs, but in his heart.

Dana moaned as she pressed herself against him, her soft curves accommodating his hard body.

He moved his hand to the back of her head and tilted it so he could better taste her even as he breathed in the scent he remembered from the night before, a light lemony scent that made him think of summer days gone by.

He left her deeply colored lips for her enticing neck and shoulder.

Her hand grasped his ass hard and his groin responded. He pressed his erection against her belly. "Dana." He spoke against her skin, his hunger for her growing.

She let go of his neck and pushed away from him,

sitting on her butt on the floor. Her breaths were quick, her hazel eyes dark, but she shook her head. "I'm not sure this is a good idea."

"Why?" He wasn't sure if it was a bruised ego on his part or her skittishness that irritated him, but this time he would get an explanation.

She didn't look at him. Instead, she pulled her legs underneath her. "Because once the arsonist is caught, you'll move on, and I don't want to get involved with someone who isn't going to hang around." She lifted her head and looked at him. "Been there, done that."

He'd never had that experience, but he could understand her hesitation better. Still, his ego wasn't assuaged. "Why do you think I'll leave after the arsonist is caught?"

She shrugged. "Because you're doing your job. When your job is over, then you'll protect someone else or go back to whatever it is you do on your two days off."

He wanted to tell her it wasn't his job to protect her, but he was sure she'd tell him to get lost and that she could take care of herself. Plus, his gut was absolutely sure she'd be pissed to learn she didn't *have* to have him for protection…legally anyway. "I'm not kissing you because it's my job. I'm kissing you because I'm attracted to you and you are to me."

She nodded, at least giving him that.

"Then there's no reason we can't enjoy each other's company like any other consenting adults."

She looked away, a sure sign she hid something else. Something that kept her from connecting with him, but was it him or a past experience that held her back?

He didn't understand this need he had to get to the core of who she was. Pushing her didn't work so well. She kept pulling back. Maybe he needed her to come to him.

Buca took that moment to rub against him. He scratched the cat behind his ear before stroking its silky back up to its tail. He watched as Buca then sauntered to Dana, rubbing against her so she would pet him as well. Hmm, maybe that's what he needed to do. Let her know he wanted her, but let her make the moves.

Pleased with his new plan of action, he rose and reached out his hand to help her stand. She didn't ignore him. He had to keep himself from pulling her against him. "I guess I should feed this feline and pack up some clothes. Would you like something to drink? I'm pretty sure I have beer and ice tea. Maybe even some cola."

She shook her head. "No, I'm good." She left the kitchen as he dished out wet food for Buca, then he filled the bowls with cat chow and fresh water.

When he walked into the living room, he found her looking at a picture of him and his family. "It was taken last year when everyone descended on my aunt and uncle's homestead in San Marcos for Christmas. We make quite a crowd."

She pointed to Lexi. "She looks like the paramedic I saw when I woke up in the ambulance."

"She is." He liked having family in town. "That's Lexi, one of my younger cousins."

"I thought two family members couldn't work in the same department." She finally looked at him. "To avoid fighting or collusion."

Collusion? He only heard that term used in the police department. "I'm only assigned to Station House 58 for a month. They had some people out on medical leave and needed help. So I'm on loan, and yes, I did volunteer. My aunt wanted me to see if my cousin's relationship with Dane Chandler was as wonderful as she made it out to be. Turns out it is." He smiled to reassure her because she looked very concerned.

She turned back to the picture. "I was an only child."

He didn't need to see her face because the tone of her voice told him she wasn't simply an only child but a lonely child. That made the death of her cat that much more devastating. He took a step toward her and stopped. "Being the oldest of four added a lot of pressure."

She looked over her shoulder at him. "Pressure?"

"Yes. I was expected to be the role model for everyone and my parents were much stricter with me." He folded his arms. "The rodeo circuit was the one way I could escape that, at least for a little while."

Her look was pensive. "I can see that. I guess I was lucky. No one was looking up to me." Her smile was short and she continued to peruse the pictures he had scattered about the room.

She picked up one of his old horse, Flint. She smiled at it, probably because there was more horse than him in that one. He was only nine. She didn't ask any questions, just put it back down.

He should go upstairs and grab a few items for staying at—he had a better idea. "Maybe you should stay here tonight."

Her gaze snapped to his. "Why would I do that?"

He shrugged, pretending it wasn't as important as it was. "I have two beds here. The one upstairs in my bedroom and the fold out one in this couch. You could take my bed and I could stay down here. That way anyone after you would have to go through me first."

"Oh." She glanced at the couch and back at him. "Okay."

Okay? Now he was completely confused. He expected a number of arguments, but he wasn't going to look a gift horse in the mouth. "Great."

~~*~~

Dana grabbed up clothes for the next day and a t-shirt to sleep in and threw them in a canvas bag while Bo waited in her vehicle outside.

She'd been surprised Bo owned a cat. Buca wasn't only well cared for, but well-loved as evidenced from Bo's patience with him, especially when the cat climbed up his jeans to get his attention. She grinned, her heartwarming as she recollected how gently Bo had pried the cat's claws from his pants and apologized for the cat's bad behavior.

It had been a wonderful afternoon. Bo had her practicing with a fire extinguisher, discovering where they were located in the buildings she was in regularly, and buying one for her apartment since hers had expired. She'd even bought two for Rainbow Acres, one for each exit as he'd taught her.

He even explained how sprinkler systems worked in buildings, what to do if she or an animal was on fire and had answered at least a hundred of her questions.

That he took her seriously and understood she wasn't some crazy woman, knocked down her trust barriers. The fact was, she trusted Bo with her life. She'd lucked out that he volunteered to protect her. Having a police officer hanging around her apartment would have been awkward at best. Bo was nothing like her father or the other police, fire and city officials who lied to her.

How many years had her father promised to take her to Sandy's bakery to pick out the biggest birthday cake they had and never did? How many times had he told her mother he had to work late and then came home smelling of scotch? The worst was when he apologized for shooting her cat and told her he'd get her two more. It was the worst because she knew he was lying, even at eight years old.

He kept them poor while he spent his salary, saying

he'd earned it risking his life and he'd spend it as he saw fit. Of course, he was just the first to lie to her.

She shook her head and shoulders in an attempt to dispel the negative squalor of her childhood. She was an adult and she made her own money and her own choices now. Bo Fletcher was a good choice as a protector.

Still, she should have her head examined for going to Bo's house for the night, but after all he'd done for her, she just couldn't make him sleep on her couch again.

Picking up the bag, she paused. She could have him sleep with her in her bed. There was no doubt they both would enjoy that, but she wasn't a casual sex kind of person. The thought of being with him and then him leaving her life when the arsonist was caught already had her heart aching.

She left her room and headed out the door. They would stop by the station so he could retrieve his truck then she'd follow him to his house. Running down the stairs, she dug out her keys to open her mailbox.

"Hey, you look like you're going out, not coming in." Jim surprised her as he stepped out of his first floor apartment.

"Are you home early?" She unlocked her box and pulled the mail out.

He joined her at the mailboxes, his forehead, which was rather high due to a receding hairline, sweaty. She'd seen him push his hair back a number of times as if his receding hairline made it so much easier to do.

He reached into his own box. "Hmm, junk, junk, junk, oh a bill. Now there's something." He snorted quietly, which was so like him. He closed his box. "How's your apartment upstairs? You need anything? A rug cleaner? I have one if you want to borrow it."

She shook her head. "No. There's a lingering smoke smell, but I threw out the rugs. I'm thinking I'm going to need to wash the walls and floors and everything else before it will be completely gone."

"I'm sorry. Is the woman across the hall from you with the yappy dog in the same situation? I haven't seen her since the fire."

She glanced up the stairs. "No, I haven't seen Tanya." *Though I certainly heard her.*

"I stopped by the hospital to see if you were okay, but you were sleeping." He looked hopeful, like he might gain brownie points from a teacher for his thoughtfulness.

"I heard." She smiled kindly. "Laura told me. That was very nice of you."

He blushed and held up his mail. "Guess I better go read my junk."

She nodded before he shuffled back to his apartment. Then she stuffed her own "junk" in her bag before heading out to her vehicle.

"Everything okay?" Bo's scowl seemed out of place as she sat behind the steering wheel.

"Sure, why?"

"That gentleman wasn't giving you any problems, was he?"

Ah, he saw Jim through the tall glass windows on each side of the door to the building. She chuckled. "Hardly. That's Jim Lawrence. He was one of my visitors while I was at the hospital." She pulled out onto the quiet street just a block off a major thoroughfare.

"He did? Hmm. What does he do for work?"

"What are you thinking? That he's the arsonist? I'll have you know that despite being in town for only three months I had two other visitors, Tanya and Laura. If you investigate Jim, then you'll have to investigate them, too."

"And me."

She glanced at him as she stopped at a red light. "And you what?"

"I visited you at the hospital too." He gave her a sly grin.

She watched the road as she drove to the fire station. "Yes, but you weren't there to see if I was okay. You were there to lecture me because I ran back for Misty." She tensed, expecting him to continue that lecture.

He surprised her. "Did the cat recover okay?"

"Yes. In fact, I'm going to see her and the Sheridans tomorrow. They are staying at Mrs. Sheridan's sister's house outside Dallas and it sounds like Mr. Sheridan is not happy." She pulled into the fire station parking lot and stopped her SUV. "I guess Mrs. Sheridan's brother-in-law expects Mr. Sheridan to pull his own weight." She grinned. "I so want to see that."

He looked at her, his green gaze alight with amusement. "You have a mean streak in you, don't you?"

She shrugged. "Maybe."

He jumped out of the vehicle and strode to his truck. She sighed. *That man has the nicest ass. And boy would I like a piece of it.*

She gripped the steering wheel. *What about not wanting to get hurt? Crapola, it was far too late for that.*

She started to fall for him the minute he kissed her in the station. When she saw he owned a cat and then he took her seriously, she fell way in over her head.

Bo pulled out and she followed him.

He's going to leave as soon as they find the arsonist. He's just doing his job. Don't be an idiot.

Bo glanced at Dana as he loaded the dishwasher. She sat at the kitchen island where they had eaten, now slowly peeling the paper off her water bottle. He could sense her nervousness over staying with him. She'd been fine during dinner, actually opening up a little about her past.

He'd learned her parents had divorced shortly after the cat episode and her mom had wanted her to quit school at sixteen, but she'd finished, working after school instead to help pay for food. After landing her first job, she'd gone to college online, finally graduating with a degree after eight years.

Dana had a way of making him look at things differently. He liked that about her. What he didn't like was that she was uncomfortable now… with him.

Part of him wanted to reassure her while the other part felt guilty she was with him under false pretenses. But he was one hundred percent positive she'd leave if she thought she wasn't required to have protection, and he was one hundred percent positive she needed it.

With the last dish loaded, he closed the machine and wiped his hands on a towel. He leaned back against the sink. "Did you like my meatloaf?"

"Huh?" She looked up at him startled. "Oh yes. It's better than I can make. Is it true firefighters are good cooks?"

He nodded. "For the most part, but it's not a hard and fast rule. I think they should add a cooking course to our degree program, even if it's an elective. We need one easy A."

Her lips quirked at that.

"Would you like to go for a swim? I don't have the hot tub running anymore, but the pool is fairly warm."

She turned her head to look out the sliding door off the kitchen. "No, I didn't bring a bathing suit."

He wished he could say she didn't need one, but that would just add to her unease. "Then why don't we bring our drinks outside and enjoy the sunset."

She raised her bottle. "I think I would like something a little stronger than this."

He nodded. Turning, he opened the refrigerator. "I have beer, wine and…well, beer and wine. Unless you consider milk stronger than water." He looked at her and winked.

It worked. Her shoulders relaxed an inch or two. "I'll have a beer."

He opened it for her, and they headed outside beneath the awning. He waited, watching the sky as it started to glow. It was still a little warm in the shade, but a light breeze blew. He took a swig of beer, hoping she'd eventually speak.

"Why did you become a firefighter?" She didn't look at him when she asked, her gaze on the horizon.

That wasn't exactly the topic he'd hoped she'd bring up. "I wanted to save people from being burned to death. I'm usually on the ladder truck, or the engine if the ladder isn't needed because my specialty is rescue."

She finally looked at him, her hazel eyes an even mix of colors in the fading light. "No, I mean why? What made you decide you wanted to risk your own life to save strangers?"

Shit, he should have known she'd want to dig deeper. If he'd been dating Mandy from the bar, he'd bet they'd be talking about the latest movie or the next band coming to town. Actually, if Mandy was here, they probably wouldn't be talking at all. He'd rather be talking to Dana than in bed with Mandy.

Despite having come to terms with it, it still scratched at the wound in his heart to relive it. He took a deep breath. "I was a teenager. Like most boys that age, I had lots of buddies, but one particular guy, Deacon, got me. We both loved riding and wanted to be bull riders."

The image that had haunted him for years rose up again, the memory refusing to fade with time. "I wasn't old enough to drive yet, so my dad took me over to Deacon's. We'd planned to go hunting for the weekend."

He forced his mouth to form the words. "We arrived at his ranch after the fire trucks."

Chapter Eight

Bo stared, seeing the entire scene, feeling the heat from the blaze. "The fire department only had the water in the engine, the tanker still on its way. Back then it wasn't automatic to send a tanker as some ranches had ponds or dry hydrants. Deacon's didn't."

Dana laid her hand on his forearm and he looked down at it, not really seeing it, but definitely feeling the comfort it offered. "The house was an inferno. I guess the old wood was a treat to the fire. It just gorged itself. Between that and the breeze, like the one right now, the fire was happy to devour everything in that house."

"Including Deacon?"

At her question, he looked at her. "Yes. He tried to get out of the house. I saw him in the bay window. He was on fire. It smothered him like a swarm of bees. No matter how he moved, it covered him. I started to run forward to help, but one of the firefighters grabbed me and wouldn't let me go. They'd seen him and turned the hoses his way, but it was too late. He didn't survive."

The rosy hue of the sunset bathed her face in pink, but her eyes had turned a smoky gray with her sympathy. "I'm sorry."

He grimaced. "They taught us to stop, drop, and roll back then, but we hadn't paid much attention. We didn't even have fire extinguishers in our house. My parents were very patient with me when I made them buy five for our own home and two more for the barn."

Her lips quirked up. "You wanted to make sure you wouldn't lose anyone else you loved."

"Yes." Her understanding caught him off guard. "Everyone else just thought I'd been too influenced by the firefighters that day, but actually I resented them for the longest time. I really thought I could have saved Deacon. I know better now. They did the right thing."

"I'm glad they kept you from being hurt, but I imagine you face that every day."

He grinned before taking another swig of beer. "Not every day. Only on the days I work."

She rolled her eyes and removed her hand from his arm.

"I'm glad I was working the day your apartment caught on fire. Or I would have never met you."

She stopped smiling. "You only met me because I went back into the Sheridans' apartment to get Misty and that pissed you off, so you had to lecture me at the hospital. I was so pissed I couldn't talk and set you straight."

"You're right." He chuckled. "I didn't know you spent your life rescuing animals, though what you did still wasn't the right thing to do."

Her eyes grew crafty. "So if this place was on fire and you weren't here, you wouldn't want me to find Buca before leaving the house?"

Damn, she was good. He loved that feline like it was his own child, but as he looked at her, he imagined her finding Buca hiding under his dresser. She'd try to move the heavy thing and pull Buca out even if fire nipped at her heels. He looked straight at her. "No. I would want you to be safe first."

She blinked, her eyes widening. When she opened her mouth to voice her next argument, he cut her off, not wanting to debate the issue.

"Then I'd run in and find the blasted cat."

She closed her mouth and grinned before taking a sip of beer.

"I meant what I said about being glad I met you." He wanted to say more, tell her he thought there could be a real relationship with her, but he swallowed his words. He needed to let her make the moves. She was like a feral cat he'd once rescued from a manhole.

"I'm glad I met you, too." Her smile remained.

That was progress. They sat in companionable silence as the pale pinks in the sky turned brighter only to be covered with dark purples and grays as the clouds blocked out the last rays of light.

When the sun disappeared, he asked her about Rainbow Acres Refuge and she talked for an hour. It also provided some interesting insights into who she was. She donated half her salary back to the ranch, didn't trust any man in authority what-so-ever, and was selfless to a fault when it came to animals.

She also revealed something that concerned him even more than the arsonist targeting her. Dana didn't worry about herself at all. To her, the only reason she existed was to rescue animals. They were her only purpose in life. She didn't even have any dreams of settling down with a man, having children and then taking in stray animals. She lived only in the present.

As a man who rescued people for a living, he understood how precious the present was, but life was supposed to be full of dreams and goals.

"So are you hoping to be Fire Chief some day?" They had moved back into the kitchen and her question caught him off guard.

He held up both hands. "Oh no. That is far more responsibility than I ever want. I would have to live with the fear of losing one of my men every day. I much prefer being one of the men." He paused.

She had opened the door on the topic of the future, so he might as well step through. "I want to have a family. That may not seem like much of a goal, but finding a woman who understands *and* can live with the risk I take every time I go to work will be difficult."

"I understand completely. Then again, that might be because I do similar work. I don't expect a man to ever accept what I do." She shrugged like it didn't matter.

He moved in front of her, not quite pinning her against the counter she leaned on. "I understand what you do. It's similar to my job. I now see that you do value human life and you are simply filling a gap that most people don't think twice about."

Her eyes lit, turning almost blue in her excitement. "Yes. That's it exactly."

He had promised himself to let her come to him, but she was like a flickering flame that could ignite or blow out. He might just need to pick her up and show her some love. He nixed the picking up part. His instinct said she'd resent him taking that much control, but he could show her some love.

He smiled, letting his admiration for her show. "You are an amazing person." He raised his finger to stroke her right cheek.

She blushed and shrugged again, but she didn't look away. "Not really. Like you said, I just fill in a gap."

He shook his head slowly as he lowered his face until he felt her quick breaths on his lips. "No. You're special. Precious."

Her lips opened to protest but he captured them with his own and kissed her, forcing his hand to no more than cup her cheek while his other remained at his side.

Her tongue met his, and he let her have her way as she explored his mouth.

Her scent of tart lemon filled his nostrils reminding him of the last time they'd kissed, and he had to stifle a groan. She grasped his waist and pulled him closer to her.

This is what he'd been waiting for. Deepening the kiss further, he ran his hand up her side and leaned his chest away to access her breast. He cupped the soft mound, rubbing his thumb across her nipple, feeling it harden through her tank top and bra.

She ran her hands to his back and pulled his shirt from his jeans. At the feel of her palms against his back, his cock reacted.

Pulling his lips from hers to allow himself deeper breaths and access to her neck, he trailed light kisses along her skin, keeping his desire in check.

Dana's hands ran up his back, kneading at his muscles, making him want to shuck his shirt, but this was about her. He lifted his hand to her shoulder and pulled the strap of her tank down then moved his finger lightly along the top of her breast.

Her pulse raced beneath his lips, so he dipped one finger between her bra and skin and stroked her nipple. She moaned and her hands burrowed beneath his jeans, grabbing at his ass.

Bo's balls tightened. He wanted this woman in so

many ways he couldn't even fathom them at the moment. Bending her farther back, he used his hand to pull her bra cup down and latched on to her nipple with his mouth, sucking.

"Holy moly that feels good." At her husky words, he smiled, keeping her hard nub between his teeth before rolling it back and forth. His cock was harder than his ax and it strained against his tight jeans.

Dana suddenly pulled her hands from his butt and squirmed to get away.

Shit.

He let her go, holding her up as she grasped his arms. "What is it?"

"I need your clothes off." Her look was so intense, his need rose hard in his groin.

He took a steadying breath. "I want yours off too, but not here. You deserve better than the kitchen counter."

Her brow knit in puzzlement.

His stomach twisted. She didn't recognize her own worth. He set her back and took her hand. "Come."

Without a word, she followed him upstairs to his room. When he opened the door, she finally spoke. "This is nice." Her surprise bothered him.

He scanned the pale gray walls with white trim. The silver and gray quilt on the bed was thick and rarely used. "What did you expect?"

She shrugged. "I don't know. A mess I guess."

He grinned, pleased that she wasn't disappointed

in the décor. "Part of our firefighter training is putting everything in its proper place. It's a habit."

She stood in front of him, but as she finished scanning his room, including his California king bed, she backed up a step.

He put his hands on her shoulders. "I think there is a place for you as well."

She turned to face him, her hazel eyes bright with uncertainty, and he let his hands drop.

Before she could say a word and put her concerns verbally between them, he kissed her with everything he felt—caring, protectiveness, desire. She tasted of beer and her own sweetness, which he craved.

She responded to his kiss, finally letting her passion gain control. Her arms slipped around him.

He broke the kiss and gazed at her closed eyes. She was everything he didn't know he needed. He wanted her in his life…always. The realization didn't scare him. Instead, a peace filled in the empty spots in his soul. He felt complete.

Her eyelids fluttered open and she looked back at him. She was strong, courageous, beautiful and intelligent. He couldn't ask for more. "Let me make love to you." His voice came out a low whisper.

She shivered slightly in his arms and licked her lips. Then she nodded once.

He grinned and swept her up into his arms.

"Ack, Bo! I'm too big."

He gently laid her down on his bed, still smiling like a fool. "How do you think I carried you out of your burning building?"

Her eyes widened. "All the way down those stairs?"

He nodded as he pulled his t-shirt over his head.

She moved her gaze from his face to his chest, his abdominals, his shoulders and arms. It reminded him of the night before when she caught him naked in her living room. There was appreciation and desire in her eyes.

She finally brought her gaze up to his. "More."

Need shot from his chest to his cock at her single word. Without hesitation, he toed off his boots, stripped his jeans and underwear before removing his socks. When he stood straight again, her gaze was sweeping over him once more.

He wanted her to want this as much as he did, so he turned around like he had the night before and looked over his shoulder, pleased to see he kept her interest. When he turned back, he set one knee on the bed beside her. "Your turn. I want to see every beautiful inch of you."

She blushed. "I'm not as perfect as you."

Her gaze fell and he tilted her chin up. "You are. You are amazing inside and out. You can't imagine how much I want you."

She glanced down at his cock, missing the true depth of his words, then she smirked. "I might have an idea."

She didn't though. He'd fallen hard and fast and he was determined to take her with him. Leaning over, he kissed her shoulder, her neck, her chest above her tank top.

Her hands ran through his short hair nudging him on.

He pulled her to a sitting position then grasped the bottom of her tank and drew it over her head. Without letting her finish taking her breath, he wrapped his arms around her and unhooked her bra, tugging it from her body as she lay back again.

Desire and uncertainty fought for supremacy in her eyes, and he silently cursed her parents for failing to love her. Despite his need to have her entire naked body against his, he stopped undressing her to pay attention to her breasts. Not that it was a hardship.

He gently caressed them, loving their light weight in his palms as he stroked her nipple with his thumb. Her nipples were large and hard, as dark as her lips and they begged for his attention.

Her hands rested on his arms as if she might stop him at any moment.

Lowering his head, he took one rosy tip into his mouth, loving the texture as he swirled his tongue around it before lightly biting with his teeth. When Dana's hands grasped the back of his head, he sucked the large nub gently at first then harder until she moaned.

He left that breast to perform the same ministrations to the other, first licking then biting and finally sucking the nipple hard enough to make her arch into him while her hands pulled his head toward her.

Licking the hard nub one last time, he moved lower, placing light kisses under her breasts, on her ribs then exploring her belly button with his tongue. He wanted her to know that every inch of her was precious. He needed her to understand that her being alive was important.

As he licked his way down to her jeans, the heady scent of her desire mixed with her citrusy fragrance, sending need rifling through him. Lifting his head away from her belly, despite her pull on him, he took a steadying breath.

He focused his attention on unbuttoning and unzipping her jeans, and her hands fell away. "Lift."

She did, pushing her hips up so he could move the pants over her hips and down her legs. Her sneakers were already off on the bed, so he pushed them onto the floor and let her jeans follow. He stood at the end of the bed and looked at her long body. "Beautiful."

"Not exactly." She pointed to a scar on her thigh. "That was a dog bite in Kentucky." She moved her hand to her left arm. "That was a barn fire in Maryland. This was a snake bite from Arizona." She'd pointed to her left ankle.

"And these." She covered her breasts. "Were just born small. You'd think with such large tips, there'd be more beneath."

He forced himself not to frown, but anger that she would think so little of herself cooled his need. "First, I love your breasts so I would prefer you don't insult them. As for your scars, they mean you've lived, had experiences, and in your case, were brave when others weren't. If you want to compare scars, I would be happy to show you every one of mine, but then we wouldn't make love for the next two hours."

Her lips quirked at that. "Point taken."

Relieved that she acceded the point, he quickly knelt on the bed and pulled her striped panties down. At his first glance of her moist folds, his desire returned full force. He knelt between her legs, fully intending to continue his trail of kisses, but her hands pulled on his arms.

"I want you." Her eyes showed that mix of uncertainty and need again, as if he would stop.

He wouldn't stop for anything, except a fire because the one burning inside him was about to explode. He would simply have to show her how much he enjoyed every inch of her after he satisfied her. "I want you more."

"I don't think that's possible."

Her husky voice and serious tone had every part of his body tensing, readying itself. "Do we need protection?"

Her brow crinkled in confusion before it relaxed. "No. I have an implant so I won't get pregnant. Are you, um…"

He smirked. "I've been tested and passed with flying colors. You?"

"Me too."

"Good because I want to feel every inch of your pussy as I slide in."

Her eyes widened at his words before they turned

dark, almost gray. "And I want to enjoy every inch of that hard cock that's brushing against my thigh."

If her words hadn't affected him so much, he'd chuckle, but they did and he couldn't wait. He wanted to make her his.

He lowered himself to his elbows and kissed her as he positioned his cock between her legs.

Dana was wet with wanting but uncomfortable at being so worshiped. She pushed the strange feeling away and focused on the mass of muscle against her. She ran her hands over Bo's biceps, loving the bulges that proved his strength. Crap, the second he'd picked her up, she'd melted.

At the nudge of his cock, she spread her legs, anxious to feel him, if he could even fit. Like the rest of him, that piece of his anatomy was large, and she wasn't immune to the anticipation of having it inside her.

She gazed into his eyes, his green gaze almost the color of an evergreen forest now. She felt his stomach muscles tense against her as he moved his hips higher to better find her opening. She lifted her own, anxious to have him.

He lowered his head, and she closed her eyes for his kiss. His tongue breached her lips at the same time his cock inched into her. As he spread her, gliding along her wet sheath, his tongue tangled with her own.

She opened her legs wider, silently inviting him home.

Bo pushed farther into her until he was totally buried inside.

She broke their kiss so she could focus on the feelings rising inside her. She'd never been so completely full. He stretched her where she didn't dare move, yet every inch of him sent tingling sensations flowing from her core to the tips of her fingers.

Taken. Wanted. Loved.

She opened her eyes to find him staring at her with so much caring that she had to blink to keep her eyes from watering.

"Are you okay?" His deep voice filled all the chips in her soul.

It was beyond intimate. "More than okay. I think I'm in heaven."

"Good, because right now we are headed for paradise."

She didn't have a chance to respond because he pulled his hips back only to slide right back in, causing tingles of pleasure to sparkle through. She grasped his head and pulled him down for a kiss, filling a strange need to be even closer.

Bo acquiesced and drove his tongue between her lips as he pushed his cock into her again. He continued to do so, his hips moving faster, beginning the friction in her sheath that stoked a fire of need.

She moaned into his mouth as she arched her breasts against his chest then pushed her own hips upward, comfortable with his largeness and wanting more.

She was greedy. She grasped his back and wrapped her legs over his waist, tilting her hips. His cock hit her cervix lightly, and she dug her fingers into his hard muscles. She broke their kiss. "Yes. More."

Her instinct that he'd been holding back was correct. As soon as she asked, his thrusts grew stronger.

She reveled in the motion of her body as it moved on the bed, back and forth, her clit against his skin as she met each of his thrusts with a tilt of her hips.

"God woman." His voice, a whole octave deeper, sent her to her peak.

"Bo!" She screamed his name as her orgasm exploded like a bomb, shards of joy slicing through her. Her whole body shook with spasms of ecstasy. He continued to pump into her, causing the fire to consume her. She held on to him with all her strength, the only solid thing in her abstract vision.

Bo shouted and warmth flooded her sheath, prolonging her orgasm as he shuddered against her.

His rhythm slowed sporadically, and she grasped him tighter, tears threatening, her emotions a mess. He was so much more than anything she'd imagined. He made her feel something she never had.

Loved.

Bo lifted his head and brushed her hair back from her face. "Hey."

She smiled tentatively. "Hey."

"Sorry that was so fast."

She raised her brow. "If that was fast, I'm not sure I could survive slow."

His grin was pure male pride. He wiggled his brow. "Just give me a minute and we'll find out for sure."

Her heart stopped at the look in his eye. *Crap, I'm falling for him and I don't give a rat's ass. I should have my head examined.* She raised her head and gave him a quick kiss on his chest, the only place she could reach. He lowered his face and captured her lips with his own.

The kiss, unlike earlier ones, was sweet and gentle, and tears threatened again. *Holy moly what's wrong with me?* Nervous at the strange feelings coursing through her, she broke away. "If you like, I'd be happy to get things started." She winked, hoping to break the serious moment.

He raised an eyebrow. "I didn't know you liked to ride."

She opened her mouth to disabuse him of his assumption that she knew how to ride a horse, when he rolled them both over, keeping them well attached at the hips. The surprise made her tense and his cock was still hard inside her.

Now she lay on top of all that strength. *Ah, he wants me to ride him. Now that I'm more than willing to try.* Carefully, she moved her legs and bent her knees. His cock in this position, even not completely hard, filled her to the end of her sheath.

He took one of her hands and kissed her palm. "Now you're in control."

He didn't smile, his implied meaning not lost on her. Again, his seriousness scared her, so she lightened the mood again. "Aren't I always?"

He nodded. "Yes, you are." He winked at her. "Now, let's see what you do with all that control."

Just as he said the words, he lifted his hips, causing his cock to hit her cervix, and she arched back.

"Whoa, hold on there." He tweaked her nipples with his fingers, and she bowed forward again. "Haven't you ever ridden a bronco?"

Her heart raced at the sensations in her body and she laughed at his sly expression. She may not know how to feel about the man, but she knew how she felt about his body. Tonight was going to be amazing.

Chapter Nine

Dana opened her eyes to the daylight streaming into the room. The giant black stallion painting on the wall reminded her of where she was and how she ended up in Bo's bed. She grinned before turning to find him gone.

Though disappointed, she didn't mind being alone to luxuriate in her memories. Crap, that man was strong. It was his strength, and his unrealistic view of her as precious, that completely suckered her in.

She stretched and found herself happily sore between her legs. It was well worth it after the heights he'd taken her to. Finally, she sat up, reluctant to get out of bed just yet, almost as if were she to start her day, everything would disappear like a dream.

"Hope you're hungry." Bo walked into the room, a loose pair of sweats dipping nicely to show off his abdominals all the way to his pubic hair. She finally focused on what he held in his hand. "What's this?"

"Breakfast, what else?" He put the tray on his dresser then added his pillow to hers and set them behind her back. "There you go." He placed the breakfast tray in front of her.

"Oh wow. Are those blueberry pancakes?" She took a deep breath to smell them even as she reached for the coffee.

"I wasn't sure if you wanted cream and sugar. I can go get some." He stood watching her.

"I'm good with black. This looks fantastic. I've never been served breakfast in bed before." She winked at him. "Better be careful, I might get used to it."

He smiled, his bright teeth gleaming as his eyes lit up. At least he didn't scare away easily.

"I can't wait to taste these." Digging the fork into the stack, she quickly cut off a bite and popped it into her mouth. "Hmmm." She closed her eyes. *Holy crap, I'm going orgasm over his food, too.*

As the mattress dipped beneath his weight, she opened her eyes.

"That's what you sounded like when I pumped into you the first time. If you keep making that noise, I'm going to have to ravish you again." His eyes gleamed with laughter, but his desire was evident in the ridge beneath his sweats.

She swallowed the luscious pancakes. "And if you keep looking at me like that, I won't be able to eat another bite."

"Like what?" He widened his eyes in innocence for a second before the devilish gleam was back in his gaze. "Maybe I should just get under the sheets in case you need any help with those moans."

"Don't you dare." She rolled her eyes at him. "I have to go to the Sheridans this morning and—"

"*We* have to go to the Sheridans this morning." He lost his smile.

She really did like his smile. "Yes, *we* have to go check on Misty, then we have to clean out the barn, pick up supplies, take two dogs to the vet, visit the ladies who make blankets for the animals, and stop in at Precious Pets this evening to pack up when my volunteers are done."

She took another bite, stifling a moan to avoid being late.

When she looked back at him, his gaze was so full of caring that she quickly turned away.

He rose from the bed and walked around to her side. "I have to admit, I've never been so busy on my days off."

"I'm sorry. As soon as the arsonist is caught, you can have your days back. Will you receive any extra days off for protecting me?"

He strode into the bathroom. "No. But that's okay. I find your work interesting."

She swallowed another mouthful of pancake as she heard the shower start. "I think yours is too."

He came out of the bathroom. "I know." He stood next to the bed on her side. "Are you done?"

She looked down at the tray. She'd eaten almost all of the pancake stack. As much as she loved them, she couldn't fit anymore into her stomach. Taking a forkful, she raised it toward him. "I can't eat another bite. Can you help?"

Bo opened his mouth and she fed him the last two pieces, the experience much more sensual than she expected.

"You have some syrup right here." She wiped at the drop on the side of his mouth with her finger until he opened his lips and sucked it in.

"Oh." The feel of his tongue circling her finger in his warm mouth had her body revving up again.

He let go suddenly and pulled the tray from her lap. "Your shower awaits." He bowed like a butler, but he was more Prince Charming to her.

She rose naked, blushing as he watched her walk to the bathroom. Once inside, she peeked her head around the corner. "Coming?"

He dropped the tray on his dresser and strode toward her. "Not yet, but you can take care of that in the shower."

She laughed then jumped into the warm spray, floating on a cloud. When Bo's large hands encircled her waist and pulled her against him, she melted into him. She'd never been so happy in her entire life. *I feel like I've just saved every pet in all of Dallas county.*

Bo's hard cock pressing against the top of her ass had

her focusing on the man behind her. She wiggled her hips and his hands left her waist.

"Keep that up and this won't last long." His deep voice in her ear sent shivers of excitement straight to her sheath.

After his slow lovemaking last night, she'd love a quick, hard one. She wiggled her hips again.

Bo's reaction was fast. In an instant, he spun them around so she faced the wall of his walk-in shower and pushed her against it. The cool tile sensitized her nipples as she let her head fall back against his shoulder.

His mouth sucked at the side of her neck while his right hand worked its way between her and the tile to explore her folds. His broad finger slipped into her opening then out to circle her clit.

She pressed against his hand, lifting her leg to give him better access, but instead of his finger, she felt him slide down her back a few inches until his cock was between her legs. His fingers moved back to her labia and spread her as he glided into her in one long stroke.

His breathing was rough in her ear. "I'm going to come inside you in about five seconds."

At his words, her sheath tightened and she tilted her hips back.

He growled and his fingers came up to her clit again as he pressed her from behind into his hand.

Pinned as she was against the tile wall, she could do nothing but enjoy, and she did.

Bo pumped into her hard, sliding her up the wall with the force of his thrusts, rubbing her breasts against the small tiles. She squeaked as her orgasm started, the multiple sensations converging in her core. He thrust twice more, rocking into her from behind, holding her in place as she splintered around him.

His shout filled her ears and brought her bliss to an apex, satisfaction filling her in the profound way it had last night, as if she finally belonged somewhere—in the arms of Bo Fletcher.

"What you make me feel." His guttural voice sent joy tingling through her like the remnants of a firework.

She squeezed her sheath, eliciting a quick inhale on his part. "I feel you. All over."

He pulled them away from the wall, but still held her pelvis to his. "Kiss me."

She turned her head and showed him with her mouth how wonderful it felt to be with him. When she released his lips, his gaze was far too serious for her.

"I think I like quickies." She wiggled her eyebrows since wiggling her hips at the moment was out of the question. The man's hold was tight.

"They do have their advantages, but only after a slow burn." He punctuated his statement by thrusting against her before pulling out.

She leaned against the wall again, too limp to wash up quite yet.

"Oh no, you have a cat to visit." Bo pulled her against

him and this time took the soap and proceeded to wash her all over. His ministrations had her moistening again, but he didn't stop to explore, which was just as well. The man was large and her body needed some time to recover.

When he was done with her, he wrapped her in a towel before jumping back in to clean up himself.

Finally feeling more like herself, she stepped into his bedroom and found her bag of clothes. Dressing quickly, she brushed out her damp hair. At least May in Dallas was warm. Her hair should be pretty dry by time they arrived at the Sheridans.

She'd just put her brush away when Bo came out of the bathroom stark naked and smelling like the musky soap he used. She smelled like it too, like him. That fact warmed her heart.

He grinned. "I'll be ready in two secs."

Oh, I don't mind. Take your time. She gazed at his muscular butt as he turned toward his dresser and took out clothes, his thigh muscles contracting with his movements. When he turned around, she let out a purely feminine sigh. *I can't believe that's all mine.*

Her heart cooled. No one said he belonged to her. *But I want him to. I want to belong to him. What if he doesn't feel the same?*

"I'm ready. Am I dressed okay to meet Misty?" Bo's innocent look, had her pushing her wishes aside.

"I think you'll do just fine." *For Misty…and for me.*

~~*~~

Bo walked hand and hand through the mall with Dana. She'd slipped her hand in his while they'd been looking at a pair of cowboy boots in a store window that he told her would look great on her.

There was a significant change in her since the day before. She'd started to relax around him then, but today had been a pleasure to spend with her. Once again he learned more about her, the most surprising fact that she had a fun sense of humor.

He actually looked forward to this pet shop visit, now that he had a feeling of how things worked. Dana wasn't just good with animals. She was good with the volunteers and owners of pets. It was only the official type people, like himself, that she was on guard around.

Lucky for him, he'd toppled that distrust, or he hoped he had.

"Hey, Dana." A man in a pair of khakis and a sport shirt hailed her.

She didn't tense, but he did, not because he was jealous of the man with the receding hairline, but because he didn't want her attention diverted from him. His shift was looming and he wanted to enjoy every minute with her.

"Oh, hi." She smiled her animal smile and he grinned inside. The animal smile was heartfelt with the critters, but when turned on people it was secretly lukewarm. "What are you doing here? I didn't think you came out this far."

The older man lifted his forearm. "I had to get a new battery for my watch. The kiosk next to the candle shop is the only one I've found who can replace it without scratching up the back cover."

"Oh. I see."

"I'll bet you're here for the pet adoption set-up. Do you ever stop working?" The man shook his head, the message clear that she shouldn't work so late.

Dana smiled a genuine smile. "I love my job, so it's not a chore."

"Wish I could say the same." He looked at his watch then back at her. "I better get going if I'm going to catch the bus home…unless you're heading that way shortly?"

"I'm afraid not. This will take a while."

The man nodded. "Okay. See you later."

"Who was that?" He had an idea, but wanted to be sure.

"That's my neighbor. Oh, I'm sorry. I should have introduced you."

"I got the feeling he'd prefer I didn't exist."

She looked up at him. "I was thinking the same thing. That's odd."

It was, but since he'd never met Jim before, he couldn't imagine why, unless the man had a crush on Dana. "So where is this pet store? I have to admit I haven't been there. And how did you get them to agree to offer Rainbow Acres pets once a week when they have their own pets to sell?"

They started walking again and she became animated. "Oh, that was all Laura. She set this up long before she hired me. It's a mom and pop chain and they decided that the products they could sell were enough to help out unwanted animals. Besides, our pets aren't always pretty, or young, or perfect, so people still buy animals from the store. We like this small chain because they are very particular about where they get their pets."

He noticed other men admiring Dana as they walked, which just made him feel luckier than ever. Looking ahead, he saw Mandy headed their way. Quickly, he pulled Dana toward a store front.

"Bo, what are you looking at?"

He focused on the display window and grinned. The red and black corset with the thong beneath would look great on Dana. "Do you like it?"

She flushed. "Those are too expensive. I'd rather spend my money on dog food for the refuge."

He met her gaze. "I mean if you received it as a gift?"

She looked at it again, tilting her head. "I don't think I'd know how to put it on."

He chuckled. Now he was definitely going to buy one for her. Glancing over his shoulder, he relaxed to see Mandy had passed. "That's okay. I like you in nothing better."

She rolled her eyes. "Come on. Enough window shopping."

As they turned the corner, he heard the short, high-pitched barks of excited critters. The front of the store had a number of large cages where dogs of all sizes barked at the people walking by…or attempting to walk by. Nine out of ten had to stop and talk to the puppies.

"Dana? Where have you been?" Dana's neighbor from across the hall stopped them in their tracks, her little dog's eyes zeroing in on him. "Are you okay?"

"Of course I am." Dana tried to release his hand, but he held her tight, earning him a look of irritation. "I was in bed the other night."

Tanya finally looked at him. "Hello. Did we meet?"

He nodded, but didn't say anything.

Dana finally relaxed her hand. "I'm here to check on the pet adoptions at Precious Pets."

"Oh, I was just in there and they do have some cuties. I really like the little Schnauzer, but Tiara didn't care for him." Tanya looked disappointed. What had Dana said? Tanya didn't have a niece?

"Are you looking for another dog?" He watched her closely and was satisfied when she grew uncomfortable.

"Oh, I just like to look, you know." She shrugged and turned back to Dana. "Will you be home later? I was thinking of going out. There's a new group playing at The Cave and I would like to check them out."

He squeezed her hand. He wanted her with him again tonight.

She caught on to his silent message. "I'm sorry. I won't be home tonight. I have other plans."

Tanya glanced at him again. "Well, I guess I can go to the club another night. I wouldn't leave my Tiara alone." She gave the dog a kiss and returned her gaze to Dana. "Let me know when you can dog-sit again."

"I will." Dana watched Tanya saunter off.

As she took a step toward the shop, he held her back. "She's hiding something."

"Like what?"

"I don't know, but I bet it has to do with her being at both the shelter you were at the other night and this pet store."

Dana's eyes revealed her mind's thoughts. "I'm not exactly quiet about the places I go. Tanya knows I save the animals at the shelter and she also knows about my pet adoption nights because I can't take care of her dog on those evenings."

He lowered his head and whispered in her ear. "But if she doesn't have a niece, why is she going to places that sell animals?"

She snapped her head toward him, her eyes wide.

He took advantage of her surprise to kiss her right there in the middle of the mall.

She blushed and pulled away. "Bo."

"Yes?" He winked at her.

She squeezed his hand. "Behave. I'm on the clock."

He sighed dramatically. "Then let's get back to work."

"Right." She looked confused for a moment then blinked. "This way."

They were three steps away from the store when an explosion sounded in the back of it. He let go of Dana's hand and ran inside. People screamed, running by him. He caught an employee on the way out. "Call 911!"

The woman nodded and pulled out her phone as she exited. He moved forward, checking all the aisles to be sure people got out. One older woman had fallen and was panicking as she tried to right herself. He helped her up and escorted her into the mall.

As soon as she was out, he ran back in. As he passed the first glassed-in area that held dogs, he noticed one wasn't barking. Instead, the little white poodle puppy stood there shaking, its rounded-eyes following him. Shaking off the puppy's unspoken plea, he moved past the glass area with the cats. Many meowed and a few scratched at their cages to get out. One furry black and white cat was curled up and sound asleep.

Smoke billowed from the back room, and he quickly closed the door, denying the fire one of its feeding elements.

His gaze fell on the fire extinguisher usually mounted next to the door. It was on the floor, spent.

Movement in the last glass room directly to his left caught his attention.

Dana! His heart stilled for a split second.

She stepped through the open door of the room with four cages. "I put the fire out here, but the back wall is hot. We need to empty that room."

Pride in her fast thinking warred with anger that she would put herself in danger. "Go, I'll get the rest."

"You will?" Her surprise tilted his emotional balance in favor of anger. "Yes. Now go!"

She did, and he ran into the room. There had to be fifteen more cages in it, mostly smaller critters. He picked up three rabbit cages and three guinea pig cages and ran to the front of the store where she took them from him.

He sprinted back. The sound of sirens coming closer spurred him on as he grabbed up six more cages. When he made it to the front, he had to skirt around the volunteers removing the animals that belonged to Rainbow Acres.

Once again he handed cages to Dana, who worked with practiced efficiency. As he turned to get the last of the animals, a hand clamped down on his arm.

"We've got this." A firefighter from another shift of Station 58 held him back.

Bo nodded. "Everyone's out. I closed the door to the back room, but the animals closest to that wall are at risk."

The man's eyes dawned with recognition. "Okay, got it." He let go and strode through the store, his partner close behind.

Dana came to stand next to him.

"They'll get the rest out." He looked at her.

She kept her gaze focused on the men. "They better."

Her attitude irritated him. "They will." He wanted to yell at her and hold her close all at once.

Suddenly, the ramifications of the explosion fully

materialized. The fire was at the store Dana always came to on Tuesday evenings. A chill swept through him. If they didn't find a legitimate reason for the explosion…

"Do you ever go in that back room?"

Dana continued to watch for the firefighters, her body clearly on alert. Not until they brought the last of the cages out and set them down in front of her did she finally address his question. "Yes."

Then she looked at him. "It's where they let us store our supplies, including our signs. I break down our display and keep it there for the next week." Her voice was flat but her eyes were wide. "I could have been back there."

He finally gave into instinct and pulled her to him, wishing he could take away her fear, wanting to protect her and for the first time, wondering if he could.

She stayed there a minute before pulling out of his arms. "I'm going to send the animals back to Rainbow Acres with the volunteers. I don't think there will be anymore adoptions tonight."

It was obvious she didn't want to think about the possibility that the pet store had been targeted because she would be there.

He let her go, but watched her as she directed the loading of the animals into vehicles. She had just started breaking down the display when the Fire Investigator and Cole arrived. The minute Cole saw Dana, he stopped.

Bo walked over to him. "She's the target. She always

comes here on Tuesday nights and goes into that back room. The explosion was meant to kill her."

"Shit." Cole shook his head. "We'll figure it out. Don't worry." For the second time that night, a fellow firefighter put his arm on him.

Bo shook it off. "Yeah, but will you figure it out in time?"

Chapter Ten

Dana parked her car on the side road to the fire station. She hated to admit it, but she missed Bo helping her all day. After another night at his house and in his bed, she had to squash the need to be with him. He'd grown on her so fast, but had been true to his word, an aberration in the sea of officials in her past experience.

When he asked her to promise to stop by, she'd wanted to blurt out yes like he'd asked her to marry him. Somehow, she just smiled and said she would. But the joy of being around him was addictive.

Excited to see him, she strode up the driveway past the ladder truck he worked. The engine was out there, too. Maybe they needed to be washed after last night's fire.

No one was around. She walked to a door she'd noticed last time she was there and hesitated. It opened suddenly and she stepped back.

"Oh, you surprised me. Can I help you?" The firefighter with dark blond hair and friendly hazel eyes smiled.

He reminded her of Bo with his build. "Yes, I'm looking for Bo Fletcher."

"Oh, you must be Dana. Nice to meet you, I'm Tory. Bo's in the shower. We just came in from a two alarm fire."

Her heart tightened. "Is Bo alright?" He seemed so capable that she hadn't really considered he could get hurt.

Tory waved it off. "He's fine. It was a storage facility of combustibles, so no one to run in and save." He grinned. "We had to work the hoses instead."

Her shoulders relaxed at the relief that surged through her body, her heart able to slow again. *Crap, I must like him a whole lot more than I thought. If this didn't feel so amazing, I'd walk away right now.*

"He should be down soon." Tory continued. "He's got truck washing duty. One of the perks of being on loan."

Obviously, the man was happy he didn't have to do it. She didn't like that. "I would think with him protecting me from the arsonist, instead of the police, the Captain would cut him a little slack."

Tory's brow furrowed. "Protection from an arsonist? No one is entitled to protection from an arsonist. Even if they were, they'd be protected by Texas Rangers, not the police. I guess you haven't lived in Dallas very long."

Her whole body froze. *Bo lied to me?*

Her heart, so open and filled with joy seconds ago, closed down hard, stopping her breath and causing her stomach to tighten unbearably.

"Hey, you okay?" Tory moved toward her.

She stepped back, throwing her arms up. *I'm an idiot! I knew better and I fell for it.*

Footsteps on the stairs behind the door sounded like nails hammered into her heart.

"Here he is." Tory turned his head and called out. "Bo, I think your girlfriend needs some help."

Girlfriend? She shook her head as Bo came out the door.

"Dana, what is it?" He moved toward her, concern in his green gaze.

She backed away, crossing her arms over her chest. "Don't. Just don't!"

He stopped. "What? What is it? Are you hurt?"

"Hah." *More than you will ever know.* "I'm done with your lies."

He looked back at Tory, who shrugged his shoulders.

Bo's voice softened. "Dana, tell me what you think I lied about."

Think? Think? Rage covered the hurt in her chest and allowed her to speak. "You told me I would need police protection if you didn't stay with me."

His gaze left hers and his whole big body seemed to deflate in defeat. It was all the proof she needed. "Don't you come near me ever again." She turned.

"Wait, Dana. I only let you believe that because I wanted to keep you safe."

She looked over her shoulder and glared. "You didn't

even know me. If you wanted a quick lay, I'm sure the blonde you had sniffing at your heels would have been happy to accommodate you." Furious, she stalked out of the station.

"Wait! That's not it!" Bo's yell did nothing but make her move faster.

Tears welled in her eyes. He'd seemed so real and honest. That's what hurt the most. She knew better than to trust an official. Her father, Detective Wilson, had been so good at that. Lying to her, his wife, his boss. When statements were made with absolute confidence and authority, he could get anyone to do anything.

She sat in her SUV and turned the key. She had to go somewhere, but she couldn't remember where. She kept seeing Bo's guilt, the image replaying in her mind, and the burn in her heart grew.

I wanted to believe him. I wanted it to be real.

The pain was too much, keeping her from any reasonable thought, so she headed for Rainbow Acres. Talking to Molly the sheep or hugging Cyclone might sooth her ache and help her grow a stronger shell.

Why do I have to live with a shell? I'm not a turtle.

Bo's gut hurt as he watched Dana walk away over Tory's shoulder. The man had stepped in front of him and he was about to deck him, when Dane grabbed him from behind. If Dane had been anyone but his cousin's fiancé, he would have been on the ground by now.

"Let her go. Even if you can fix this, it won't happen if you try right now. She's pissed. Wait until she has time to cool down. Your chances will be better."

He growled at Dane. "You know this from experience?"

The man backed away. "Hey, just some friendly advice for my future in-law is all." He motioned to Tory. "Leave him. He has to figure this out for himself. Let's get some chow. I'm starving."

Bo rubbed the back of his neck. Fuck. Now she thought everything they had was a lie. He had to get her back and in the meantime keep her safe.

He had planned to tell her about the Fire Investigator's findings. The explosion at the pet shop was definitely arson. If it was the same arsonist, he'd learned a thing or two since the first fires.

He couldn't lose her. He loved her. If he'd had any doubt about that, it disappeared the second she walked away with his heart. He needed them both back.

"Shit." He couldn't even think straight. Pulling his phone from his waist, he dialed Cole. "Hey, can you stop by?"

"Already on my way. I have a theory on who the arsonist is. See you in ten."

Bo hung up and walked out into the sunlight of the warm May day. People strode down the sidewalks, anxious to get wherever they were headed. Cars jockeyed for position on the busy street. Even the pigeons fluttered on rooftops waiting for a stray potato chip or bread crumb from a patron of the sandwich shop across the street. They all acted as if today was like any other day.

But it wasn't.

He felt like he was at his own point of origin and his entire body was about to burst into flame. He'd finally found the woman he wanted in his life and because he wanted to keep her safe, he'd lost her.

No fucking way. He would get her back. First, he had to keep her safe whether she wanted him to or not.

Cole's truck pulled into the parking lot.

Bo strode toward him, determination burning through him. "What do you have?"

"I'm good. How about you?" Cole's raised eyebrows made him feel like an ass, but he didn't care.

"I'm in hell right now and I'm hoping you can pull me out."

"What happened?"

Bo kept his explanation short and to the point.

"Shit. Sorry about that. I forgot I was in Texas when I told her she'd needed police protection."

"It's not your fault." Bo sighed. "I wanted to keep her safe."

"I got that and I agreed with you. We were both right."

Bo tensed. "Is it the dog fighting ring she shut down?"

Cole shook his head. "No. I looked into that angle and those men are currently serving time."

"Really? For dog fighting?" He didn't think the police looked at that kind of crime so seriously.

"No. After they lost their dogs, they thought it would be entertaining to pit teenage boys against each other. They offered a cash prize and the kids beat the hell out of each other. When they ended up at the hospital a few too many times, the police caught on."

Sometimes it was hard to keep his faith in humanity, especially with scum like that around. No wonder Dana preferred animals and had little faith in officials. After all she'd seen with the animals she'd rescued—

"I have it narrowed down to two people." Cole continued. "Amanda Switzer and Jim Lawrence."

Amanda? Oh, Mandy. "Why those two?"

"First, that chance meeting at Johnny's Sport's Pub was not chance at all. It turns out you have a stalker."

"What?" He thought back to his meeting with Mandy. "If you mean because she came to the station the day Dana was here then I wouldn't call that stalking."

"It's a lot more than that. She's been posting on social media about her firefighter boyfriend and she has photos of you at Dana's apartment fire, the shelter fire and the pet store fire."

"Fuck. But I thought women aren't arsonists."

Cole's look turned smug. "Usually, but seventeen percent of arson fires are set by women. Part of what I've learned in this arson course."

Great, so he had a stalker who might be endangering

Dana. If that was the case, he needed to stay away from her. "Wait, what about Tanya then? She lied about getting a dog for her niece as a reason for being at the shelter. Could she be part of the seventeen percent?"

"No." Cole chuckled. "I found out why she lied and it wasn't hard. She's not a quiet woman and when I went to question her, she was on her phone and signaled me to wait. Turns out, she wants to get another dog for her Tiara, but the landlord only allows one pet. She told her mother if she ever got caught with it, she'd just claim it was Dana's."

"Damn. So once again, Dana is on the short end of that proposition. So what about Jim Lawrence?"

Cole wiped his brow and started to walk toward the garage. "He's been at all the fire scenes, but I can't find a motive. He seems to like Dana."

Bo's protective instincts went into overdrive at the mention of another man liking his woman. "I knew I didn't like him. Since he's a man, isn't he your prime suspect?" They'd reached the shade of the garage and Bo led Cole toward the back.

"He would be if he had a car."

Bo opened the door to a small fridge the guys kept in the garage for water and handed Cole one. "But you said he was at every fire scene. I saw him at the mall and it was his apartment building that burned, but what about the shelter? He was there?"

Cole took a swallow than capped the water. "He

was, but he didn't arrive until the fire was contained. An arsonist likes to see his work."

"But how did he know it had happened? For that matter, how did Mandy know to come to the fires I worked? Or has she gone to all of them?"

"We think she has a scanner. Either that or a friend in dispatch."

That sounded more like the woman. "Is there anything I can do to get her off my case?"

"Not really." Cole frowned. "Until she threatens you, you really can't get a restraining order. If she's really unbalanced, then your relationship with Dana could be what is setting her off. She may want Dana dead whether you know she exists or not. If she's just desperate, then she may not be setting the fires and we're back to Jim."

Damn, he hated that he might be endangering Dana, but the need to be near her to protect her wouldn't go away. "So if I stay away from Dana, it might keep Mandy from setting more fires, but if it's Jim then I'm leaving her wide open."

Cole pointed at him with the water bottle. "You'd be better off sticking close no matter what. We are working with the police, but since nothing important has burned like a bank or a government building, it's not a top priority."

Bo rubbed the back of his neck. "She's really angry. It won't be easy to stay nearby. I'll basically have to stalk her."

"Then do it. Either that or get her to forgive you. That explosion at the mall was well planned, but the arsonist had to set it off. Next time, he or she might have figured out how to detonate remotely."

"Shit."

"Tell her it was my fault. I forgot which state I was in, which is the truth."

He shook his head. "No. I'm not blaming you on this one. I made my own mess. I'll clean it up."

"Good luck. In the meantime, I'll see if I can't find something to point toward who our culprit is."

Bo walked Cole back to his vehicle. "Thanks for coming by. How much longer will you be in town?"

"Not much. I leave the end of the week, but don't worry. This is my top priority. This and passing the final exam." Cole grimaced. "I could really use Lacey to help me with that, but she's working, so I'm on my own."

"I appreciate all you're doing. I know the Fire Investigator wouldn't be nearly as concerned." He never thought when he and Cole Hatcher landed in the same hospital room over ten years ago that he'd need his help to save the woman he loved. "If you want help studying, just let me know and I'll do whatever I can."

"Thanks. I may just take you up on that." Cole strode to his truck.

Bo watched as his friend drove away. As soon as he got off shift, he had a woman to find and convince that he only wanted to protect her because he loved her.

~~*~~

Dana ignored the buzz on her phone as she lugged the bag of feed to the barn for Molly. Bo kept leaving messages. It had been two days and she'd ignored them for a whole day, but this morning she listened to them.

Every single one.

Now she ignored his calls because she was afraid she'd cave in and forgive him. Maybe she wanted to too much. Her feelings for him were stronger than she'd thought. It wasn't until he broke her trust that she understood exactly how far she'd fallen.

But she swore she'd never be like her mother, living in a dream world only to be tossed aside when something better came along. She had her eyes wide open.

Yeah, even with them open and knowing how officials lie, I still tripped head over heels into love with Prince Charming.

As she opened the barn door, both animals lifted their heads. Molly greeted her with a "baah" hello and Cyclone came up to the stall door to see her. She dropped the feed and gave Molly a rub on her head before moving down toward the back where Cyclone nodded at her.

"Yes, I have an apple for you. Just don't tell Laura I gave it to you. She'd have my head. I think you deserve a treat once in a while."

Cyclone nudged her shoulder and lifted his head, refusing to be stroked until he had the sweet he smelled in her shirt pocket. Pulling it out, she handed it to him. "Sure. I know how important I am to you. If I didn't bring you food, then you wouldn't know I existed."

She stilled. She hadn't given Bo anything, but he'd known she existed. She'd like to say he only wanted sex, but that was a lie. She'd kept him at arms-length as much as possible. Yet he'd listened to her and opened his mind to her passion. Crap. Was her own past barricading her way?

She shook her head as she opened the sheep's food bag and scooped it out for her. The fact was, he still lied. He may have had good intentions…she dropped the scoop in the bag. Her father never had good intentions.

He treated her and her mother like criminals, always trying to trip them up, always lying to make himself seem even more important. Telling them how he'd caught a murderer because he was a bad ass then they'd see the officer on the news who had actually made the arrest, her father nowhere in sight.

Bo had never done that, never pretended to be something he wasn't. He never promised something he didn't give. She pulled her phone out of her pocket.

One message.

She couldn't resist listening.

"Dana, I'm sorry. I'll say that for the rest of my life if I have to just to have you forgive me. I thought I was keeping you safe, but I understand that was your choice. I'm weak when it comes to you. I don't want anything to happen to you. I'm concerned. It's been two days without a fire. Cole says that means the next one will be big. Please. Call me."

Shootin' sheepherders, how am I supposed to resist that? She looked at Molly. "Do you think I should forgive him?"

The sheep continued to chow down, completely ignoring her. "I know. It's my problem and I need to solve it. As soon as I finish the feedings, I'll call him. Can't hurt to talk. Maybe then I can figure out what to do."

Cyclone whinnied.

"So you agree with my plan, big man?" She closed up Molly's feed bag, but as she tied it off, the horse whinnied again and his hooves hit the stall door, rattling the crowbar. "What is it, Cyclone?"

She left the feed bag and walked toward him. He backed up for another run at the door. "Whoa, wait. It's okay. What's the problem?" She looked in his stall to see if there was a bee or something, but had to stand back as he pawed at the door again. Luckily, it held… but barely.

She lowered her voice. "It's okay, sweetie." She searched for the cause of his agitation, but couldn't figure out what the problem was.

She took a deep breath, ready to try and sooth the horse again when she smelled it.

Gasoline!

The next moment the doors to the barn exploded and she went flying.

~~*~~

Bo heard the explosion from the other side of the rambling home known as Rainbow Acres. Dialing 911 as he left his truck, he ran to the house. From his side, he didn't see any fire or smoke, but Dana had gone in there and he had to get her out.

His heart beat twice as fast as he yanked open the front door. He'd followed her for the last two days, afraid something like this would happen. Racing through the home filled with agitated animals, he yelled. "Dana!"

He could barely hear himself among the noise of barks, meows and bleats. She wasn't there, nor was the fire. It had to be at one of the outbuildings. Running back outside, he rounded the corner and saw the blaze. No!

Movement in his peripheral vision caught his attention. He turned to find Jim throwing down an empty gas can and lighting a pipe bomb. In a split second, his mind registered the smell of gasoline as he'd left the house. The man had poured it from the front door to halfway around the side, intending to burn the animals alive to get to Dana.

Without another thought, Bo ran at the surprised man and tackled him to the ground. The lit pipe bomb rolled against the house. Fuck.

"Get off me! I'm not hurting anyone!"

"You fucking bastard! Dana's in there!" He punched

the surprised man in the face, knocking him out. Then he jumped off.

The gasoline had lit immediately and flames lapped at the two walls. He let it burn. He had no idea what fire station had this district, but he hoped they arrived soon.

He had to save Dana.

Dana landed on the bales of hay at the back of the barn. Tiny flames flickered near her. Jumping up, she turned. She thought the fire at her apartment was hell. This one was far worse. The doors of the barn were gone, leaving an opening surrounded in fire.

Cyclone screeched and pounded at his stall door. She ran to him. Fire covered his side.

"No." Spying a horse blanket that had been blown to the floor, she grabbed it up. She only had one chance at this. Before she lost her nerve, she pulled the crowbar from the stall door and stood to the side.

Cyclone battered the door and as it opened, she threw the blanket over him. He galloped straight outside, the blanket already starting to fall off.

She stepped forward to follow him when a piece of the roof fell, catching her on the back and throwing her down. Fire scorched her and she screamed.

Pushing the board off, she rolled onto her back like Bo had taught her. It hurt like hell but the burning stopped spreading. Rolling back over on to her hands and knees, she took short steadying breaths, not willing to breathe too deeply. She started for the opening, wishing Laura had thought to put a back door on the barn.

She kept low as Bo had reiterated. If she could just see him again. She'd tell him she loved him. He'd been right. She had needed protection and she had been too stubborn to accept it graciously. Oh God, she wanted to see him, hold him, make love again.

Tears clouded her vision as she crawled around burning hay, her back sending jolts of pain with every movement. As the heat built, her need to escape spurred her on. For the first time in her life while she was in danger, she thought of herself. She wanted to live. She wanted to see Bo.

Another piece of roof landed on her burned back and she screamed again, fighting the blackness of unconsciousness as the pain took her breath away.

But the darkness was so enticing.

Bo sprinted past the dog kennels, their barking making it hard to think. Luckily, he only had one thought on his mind. Save Dana. As he came closer to the completely engulfed barn, the roof collapsed.

A scream split the air over the roar of the fire.

"Dana!" He ran into the yawning opening engulfed in flames. In front of him was the burning wood of the roof. Heedless of the fire, he threw back one board after another. Six feet into the mess, he grasped her.

"Bo?" Her voice was weak.

He let his training take over, carefully extracting her from the burning roof. He hauled her over his shoulder and crouched low as he made his way out of the barn. He dropped to his knees a safe distance away and lowered her to the ground.

She screamed as he laid her on the grass and he quickly rolled her over.

"Holy shit." Her shirt was gone and her back was a puckered mess. "Dana, you're going to be okay." His heart lodged in his throat. *Please let her be okay.*

"Bo?" She lifted her head to see him.

"I'm right here." He felt the sting of tears. He could lose her. Where was the damn fire engine?

Her pain-filled gaze moved past him and her eyes widened. She coughed as she tried to speak. "The house." She coughed again. "The animals." Tears flowed from her eyes and he looked back to see the walls burning high.

"Please." She grabbed his forearm, her grip hard. "Save them. Caged. Helpless."

"I can't leave you."

Her fingers bit into his skin. "Must. Love you, but will hate you."

She loved him? Elation warred with fear, but he had no time to understand exactly what he felt. Her nails scratched him hard.

"Go." She scowled at him, her eyes filled with fear, not for herself, but for the tiny creatures in the home.

He wished Lexi were here to take care of Dana. "I'll

go, but you have to promise to stay awake until I come back."

She smiled weakly. "I will."

He'd seen the number of animals in those rooms and there was no way he'd be able to move them all to safety. His only option was to put out the fire.

Leaving her killed him, but if the animals in the house died, it would kill her.

He ran back to the house, calling 911 again to request an ambulance. Racing through the front door, he grabbed the fire extinguisher he'd noticed on his way in. He noticed it because it was new and not mounted yet. One of the purchases they had made for Rainbow Acres.

He ran back outside and sprayed the base of the fire on one wall as far as the extinguisher held out. Even if he could just slow the fire down until the engine arrived that would be enough. Shit, they weren't exactly in a neighborhood and laying down a line wouldn't be an option. He hoped they brought a tanker.

Running to the other side of the house, he stopped to roll Jim farther away from the flames. The man remained unconscious which meant Bo didn't need to waste time tying him up.

He unraveled the garden hose and put it on full blast. Spraying a gas fire of this size with a garden hose wouldn't put it out, but it could slow it down. He focused on the other wall, making the fire work for every inch of fuel it wanted to consume.

Finally, sirens sounded in the distance and relief barreled through him. As soon as the fire trucks were in sight, he dropped the hose and sprinted back to Dana.

Her eyes were closed.

His gut tightened as he fell to his knees in front of her. He swallowed down the lump in his throat, his chest so tight he could barely get the words past his lips. "You promised."

Her eyelids didn't even flicker. "I'm awake. My eyes hurt. Did you save them?" Her words, barely audible, enabled him to breathe again.

He glanced back at the flickering flames. The fire station had brought a tanker and would finish the job he started. "Yes. The rest of the fire is being doused now." He took her hand in his, unable to keep from touching her one more minute.

"I love you, Dana. You have to get better so I can show you how much I love you."

Her mouth quirked up just a bit. "You already did."

Epilogue

Dana sat on the stool at Bo's kitchen counter in a halter top, her go-to clothing these days because it was the easiest to wear with no back. This one was particularly nice because Bo had bought it for her and the material was extra light and soft.

Her very own Prince Charming came in from showing Cole the pool. "So they found enough evidence to convict him?"

Cole closed the door behind them. "Yes. Jim Lawrence will be going away for a long time. A lot had to do with your testimony. I knew he was involved, but I hadn't thought he'd rent a car just to set a fire. The man doesn't even have a real license."

"I didn't like him from the start, but that's never enough to convict someone." Bo came by and kissed her on the cheek before moving to the fridge to take out a beer with his left hand, his right still healing from his own burns. He handed the bottle to Cole then looked at her. "Would you like another?"

She held up her half-finished beer and shook her head. "Did Jim ever explain why he was so intent on killing animals? Or more specifically, the animals I helped?"

Cole pulled up a stool. "I think it was your neighbor's dog. His apartment is right beneath hers and in addition to the barking, I guess the dog ran around all night. The guy was probably sleep deprived and couldn't think straight. He knew you worked with animals, so by following you and knowing your routine, he was guaranteed to find places that had a lot of them."

Bo stood near her but only took her hand, always sensitive to her burns. "He didn't do a very good job if he was trying to rid Dallas of pets. He failed at every attempt."

"Except one." She looked at Cole. "Molly was killed by the explosion. Actually, two. Though Cyclone is alive, his scars are going to make it impossible to find him a good home. As if his penchant for kicking wasn't bad enough, he now looks awful on one side. Laura is worried about how she can keep him."

"I'll take him." Cole's offer surprised her.

"In Arizona?"

He glanced at Bo. "You didn't tell her?"

"Tell me what?" She frowned at Bo.

He gave her hand a reassuring squeeze. "Cole is not only a firefighter, but he owns a horse rescue ranch. He takes in all kinds of horses. When and if they're ready, he sells them to good homes."

She sighed in relief, the problem of what to do with

Cyclone had weighed heavily on her mind since the barn fire. "That's perfect. He's not ready to travel yet, but the vet we have is very good. Maybe by next month. How can we get him to you?"

Cole raised his bottle and gestured toward the driveway. "I'll just come back with my trailer. It will give me a chance to visit Dallas again."

She smiled. "I'd love that. You did so much, keeping Bo in the loop. If he hadn't been at Rainbow Acres…"

Bo kissed her temple. "But I was."

She swallowed back the fear that still plagued her at night and gazed at him, his green gaze comforting. "And you saved all the animals." She looked at Cole. "Would it be possible for us to visit Cyclone at your ranch?"

"Of course. Lacey and I would be happy to have you. And you would get along great with my cousin's girlfriend, Whisper."

"Whisper? That's an odd name."

"I know, but it fits her. She's an animal whisperer. She's already helped us out with a few horses and one stubborn coyote."

Dana liked the woman already. "That sounds intriguing. I look forward to meeting her."

Bo put down his beer. "Now I just need to take care of my stalker."

Cole laughed. "Actually, you don't."

Oh yes, he does. She wasn't having some woman salivating after her man. "Why not?"

"She's moved on." He kept grinning. "It appears that with Bo out on medical leave, something Captain Stewart is not happy about, by the way, Mandy needed someone else for her social media boyfriend."

Before she could ask, Bo did. "Who?"

"Rick."

Bo laughed.

She loved that sound. "Why is that funny?"

Cole lifted his beer in salute. "Rick is a lady's man. Mandy is going to have to work hard to get a photo of him without another woman on his arm."

"Oh. I guess that is fitting in an ironic way."

Bo clinked beers with Cole. "In a *good* way. Maybe they will teach each other a lesson."

Cole took a sip and put his bottle down as he lost his smile. "I need to apologize to you, Dana."

"You do?" She'd hardly been around him long enough in the last couple weeks for him to have done something to apologize for.

"I do. I was the one who told you that you would need police protection from the arsonist. I wasn't being a jerk. I truly felt we needed to keep you safe." He looked at Bo.

She tilted her head so she could gaze at the man who loved her enough to risk himself to save her. "There's nothing to forgive. If you hadn't, I'm absolutely sure I would have died in the shelter fire or the mall fire."

Bo's relief was obvious in his gaze and this time she squeezed his hand.

Cole cleared his throat. "Well, I should probably hit the road. I've got a long drive and Lacey said she had a surprise for me."

From the man's secret smile, she had a feeling it might involve the bedroom. He bent down and kissed her on the cheek. "Take care of yourself and him." He pointed to Bo.

"I'll do my best."

Bo left to walk Cole out, but she wasn't alone. Buca jumped down from the bay window seat and rubbed against her legs. "Oh sweetie, I can't pick you up."

"I'll get her for you." Bo strode in and lifted the sleek black cat onto her lap. She scratched him behind his ears, which caused him to purr.

Bo stroked the cat as well. "Why don't *you* own an animal. With your interest in their welfare, I'm surprised you don't have one."

She took her gaze from Buca and met his. The image of Zorro lying motionless in her backyard flashed through her mind. "I didn't want my heart ripped out again."

Bo stopped stroking Buca and lifted his good hand to her cheek. "What your father did was wrong in every sense. But you're right. Our animals don't live as long as us, but I think they deserve to be well cared for while they are here and you would definitely do that." He watched her for something, but she had no idea what.

If he expected to talk her into adopting a pet, he would be disappointed. "I agree, which is another reason

I've never owned a pet because I didn't have enough time to give an animal the attention it deserved."

He grinned, raising one eyebrow. "Well, you do now, so you better get used to it."

She frowned not sure what he meant until he dropped his gaze to her hand, which rested on Buca's back, the cat already asleep on her lap. "But he's your cat."

"Not anymore. Now he's *our* cat. You're going to have to share in cleaning his litter box, learn when he can have his banana ice cream, and let him sleep on your lap while you watch a movie. You have no choice. You will have to move in with me and help me take care of him."

Joy burst through her chest, causing her eyes to water. "Really?"

His face turned serious. "Dana, I love you. I want you with me night and day. And when I can't have that I want to come home to you or meet you at the mall to take down adoption signs or help you transport baby rabbits or—"

She put her finger over his lips. It was as if her whole life had led up to this very moment, a moment she wouldn't trade for anything. *Holy crapola. I really did find my Prince Charming!* She spoke softly, unable to believe this was for real. "I'd be honored to be Buca's mom."

Bo's smile warmed her heart and as his lips descended on hers, he lit a flame that would consume them both… *in a good way.*

Read on for an excerpt from Logan's Luck (Last Chance #4)

Chapter One

"What the hell is she doing here?" Logan Williams looked up from where he knelt on the barn floor to scowl at the local vet.

His brother stepped up next to her. "Dr. Jenna's here to help."

He glared at Trace. "I don't remember asking for any help."

"You never do. Maybe if you did, life would go a little smoother for you." He grinned. "Now, no fighting while I'm gone." Trace winked then turned on his heel and strode out of the barn whistling.

Damn troublemaker. It was just his luck that when he moved to the Last Chance horse rescue ranch, his extended family had retained the services of Dr. Jenna Atkins, local vet and former one-night-stand. She was the only woman he'd fought the urge to call for a month before their night together was finally put to rest where it belonged. "Well, since you're here, you might as well make yourself useful. Go to the house and get me a couple bottled waters. This is going to be a while."

The five-foot four-inch woman in a white button down collared shirt and snug blue jeans crossed her arms over her bountiful chest. Her blue-green eyes sent need spiraling up his spine, despite the anger in them. "Let's reverse that, shall we? Since I'm the medically trained vet," she lifted her large leather bag of medicines and equipment, "I suggest you go get *us* some waters and I'll take mama's vitals. What's her name?"

He ground his teeth at her logic, trying to find a way around it. He couldn't. "Her name is Macy."

Jenna opened the stall door and walked in crooning to the horse, who, damn her, nickered at the vet. Jenna stood right next to him and set her bag on the concrete floor. "You're in my way."

Swallowing a completely inappropriate response, he rose to his feet, purposefully towering over her. "I'll be right back." His words came out like a threat, but he didn't care. Brushing by her, he exited the stall and stalked out of the barn.

Thoroughly pissed off, he swore if he ran in to Trace he would lay him out cold. Ignoring the final reds and purples in the darkening sky, he took the three steps to the porch and threw open the front door. The screen banged against the doorframe as he stalked down the hall to the kitchen.

When he stepped into the room, he halted at his grandmother's scowl. "Don't you go slamming my doors. How old are you? Thirteen?"

It wasn't his grandmother's scolding that calmed him so much as it was his sleeping fifteen-month old daughter in his grandmother's arms. "She's getting too big for that, Gram. Here, let me put her in our room."

She looked down at his daughter and her scowl faded. Charlotte had that effect on everyone who helped out at the ranch. Despite how rambunctious she was while awake, everyone doted on her.

When she slept, you'd think she was the Queen of Sheba the way they all tiptoed around the ranch house. The thing was, Charlotte was as likely to sleep at mid-afternoon as at night, her schedule like that of a puppy, which unfortunately, gave him little sleep. Luckily, the night sleeping had improved.

"She'll never be too big for my arms." His grandmother practically crooned her words.

"Come on, Gram. I bet your left arm is completely numb now. Let me take her up."

His grandmother nodded, and he lifted his daughter into his arms. As he turned away to head upstairs, he caught his grandmother in his peripheral vision, shaking out her arm.

He didn't say anything as he turned the corner and climbed the stairs. Everyone in the house, which luckily was just his grandparents and himself now, doted on his daughter.

When he'd first arrived, a new single dad without a home, the place was bursting at the seams with Cole and old Billy, not to mention Cole's now wife Lacey. Since his cousin, Cole, jointly owned the horse rescue ranch with their grandparents, Logan really couldn't say anything. Then his brother Trace had shown up during his divorce and getting sleep had been more a wish than a reality.

At the top of the stairs, he turned left and brought Charlotte into his room with the two twin beds. Next to one of them was Charlotte's crib. There was an empty room across the hall, now that everyone had moved out, but he wasn't quite ready to have his daughter that far away from him. The small bedroom at the end of the hall his grandfather was renovating, so it was unusable.

Gently, he laid Charlotte down, her little hand still holding her teddy with the cowboy hat. His grandmother had insisted that she have a horse as soon as she could crawl, even if it was a stuffed one, but that animal remained in the crib all day while the teddy went everywhere.

He gazed down at his daughter, still amazed that she was really his. Despite all his precautions, all his maneuverers to avoid any kind of entanglement with a woman beyond a quick night of sex, something had failed. At first, he thought it was just more of his perpetual bad luck, but having Charlotte in his life had changed everything…except his luck.

He brushed her thick brown hair, kept short after she started chewing on it. He'd had to cut his own hair short after she pulled it one too many times, leaving sticky syrup in it that would have taken days to wash out.

He still didn't know anything about being a dad. All he had to go on was what he remembered with his own father, who he admired most of his life…until the end just before he passed. That's when his bad luck had really started.

Thanks to his grandparents though, he was learning a lot more about being a parent and especially about being a parent of a little girl. Hopefully, she'd have better luck and be more successful than he ever was.

Turning away, he gazed at her from the doorway then turned off the light. A little pony nightlight illuminated the floor so he could find his way to his bed once it was dark. He chuckled silently as he descended the stairs. He would have been mortified if his mother had put a nightlight of any kind in his bedroom when he was a boy. He'd been tough, but Charlotte was soft and sweet.

Entering the kitchen, he found his grandmother had moved to another room, so he opened the fridge, grabbed four bottled waters and headed back outside. He wasn't about to tell Jenna, but he was worried about Macy.

When he approached the stall, he heard Macy whine. Damn, he was right, it wasn't going well. He set the water bottles on a beam and leaned over the stall door, in no hurry to get into such a confined space with Jenna. "What's wrong?"

She didn't look at him. "The foal's legs are both coming out at the same time. That won't work. We need to get her up and walking or you could lose both of them."

"Fuck." He pulled open the stall door, his aversion to Jenna forgotten in his concern for Macy.

"Help me get her up."

"Up? She's trying to give birth." He looked at the small legs sticking out the vulva. "If we get her up, the foal might fall back in."

Jenna finally gave him her undivided attention. "That's what I'm hoping."

"What?"

"Listen, if we don't get her up and walking around, you're going to have one dead foal and one sick mama. Darn it, I wish I had Whisper here. At least she'd help instead of question everything I say."

He'd been about to argue, but at her last comment he shut his mouth and moved toward the horse. His brother's girlfriend, Whisper, was amazing with animals, but she was a bit odd. That Jenna would prefer her over himself irritated him, motivating him to show he could help.

With a few coaxing words and a push in the right direction, they got Macy up on her feet again. As he expected, the foal's feet disappeared into Macy.

"Now we need to walk her." Jenna issued orders like she was born to it, which rankled. He was the one who had run a ranch before. *Yeah, and what a mess that was.*

Swallowing his pride, he grabbed a halter. He hoped she knew what she was doing. He'd only had one mare in his lifetime have a difficult birth and they had lost the baby. At the time, it was all they could do to save the mother. Now, he couldn't imagine losing the foal. Must have something to do with being a parent himself.

Jenna walked Macy down to the opening of the barn and back a few times, then she handed him the leads. "Hold those for a moment."

He did as instructed, determined not to say a word. If he did, it wouldn't be helpful, of that he was sure. His gut felt like a bulldozer ran through it.

Jenna moved her hands over Macy's enlarged abdomen then she looked up at him. "Lead her into the stall. I think the foal has moved and Macy is not going to wait much longer. I just hope it has moved enough."

He led Macy inside to the fresh hay he'd put down when he'd noticed her condition. Quickly, he removed the halter. "Okay, Macy. It's up to you now, girl. Don't let me down."

Macy stood still as they backed away, then slowly lowered herself to the floor of the stall again and rolled on to her side. She started to breathe heavy and then the contractions began.

"Here we go. Cross your fingers, pray, or just hope that the foal exits correctly this time, or I will have to perform a cesarean in not so sterile conditions."

"Can't you do something to increase the odds in her favor?" She was a vet after all. "Like drugs or something?"

She frowned at him but turned her attention back to Macy when the horse whined. She spoke quietly. "Do me a favor and stay out of the way."

He ground his teeth to hold in his response. For Macy's sake, he'd step back, but after this, the woman would be getting an earful of opinion from him whether she wanted it or not.

The first hoof appeared enveloped in the white birthing sac. That was a good sign. Another couple heaves on Macy's part and another foot appeared slightly behind the first. *Yes! Come on, Macy!* The next part was critical. *Come on girl. Let's see the head.*

Logan gripped the top of the stall door, his heart beating as if he'd just galloped across the valley and back. He must be getting too old for this because he'd never been this tense with a birth when growing up on his family's ranch.

The mare chuffed and whined as two more contractions hit her. They were very rhythmic so that was good, but he glanced at Jenna and the concern on her face made him want to yell.

Another two heaves of the mare's sides and more of the white sac slid out onto the new hay. He stepped forward only to find his way blocked by a stiff arm.

"Stay out of my way." Jenna moved past him and with practiced precision, slit the white sac to reveal the foal's head. She delicately cleared the animal's orifices before she stepped away again. At the smile on her face, his entire insides relaxed.

Macy gave another whine and the foal spilled out, except for its hind feet. Jenna glanced over at him and nodded, her lips still curved in the joy of a new birth.

At that moment, in the dimly lit barn, she looked like

an angel. Her thick brown hair pulled back away from her face, emphasized the flush of her cheeks and the soft curve of her neck. In her happiness, her blue-green eyes almost sparkled.

It took everything he had inside him to stay where he was and not pull her into his arms and kiss her. She made it worse by walking over to him, keeping herself far from Macy and the new foal, who was not yet completely out of its mom's body but would be soon.

"She should be fine, but I'll check them both in about twenty minutes." She kept her voice low, like she had when they were in bed. "It'd be best if we left them alone right now."

He stared at her. He should open the stall door for her, but if he moved his arm, it would wrap around her of its own accord. He couldn't allow that, but he wanted it so much he couldn't think straight. "Jenna."

His voice was husky with his own need.

Her brows knit together in puzzlement. "What? Do you have something you want to say?"

Yes! I want to tell you I want you so much I'd take you right here in the next stall. Instead, he swallowed hard against his own weakness. "I can take it from here."

She frowned as she pulled the stall door open just far enough to slip out before holding it for him. "We can discuss that once you get out of there."

There was nothing to discuss. He'd lived on a ranch his whole life. He could take care of a new born foal, dammit. *Yeah, but you also lost the ranch, so what does that say about your expertise, smart ass?* He stalked through the opening then spun around to confront her.

She quietly latched the stall door. Without turning to look at him, she strode toward the barn exit.

Oh no, she wasn't getting away that easy. He caught up to her just before she reached the open barn doors and grabbed her arm. "There is nothing to discuss. I'll take care of the foal and Macy."

At her surprised look, he lowered his tone. "I didn't call you."

She pulled her arm away. "No, you didn't. You're not very good at that, are you? Returning calls isn't one of your talents, is it?"

It didn't take a brain surgeon to figure out she was talking about the days after their night together when she called him and he didn't return her calls. When he lived near Catalina, he thought someone like her from out of town would be easier to keep away. Joke was on him. He cracked two of his knuckles against his thigh. "Listen, it's just that—"

"Oh, spare me the excuses. We both know I was just some easy lay for you." She stepped closer to him, staring him down even though she was at least ten inches shorter than him. "For your information, I don't do one-night-stands. There was nothing easy about it for me."

Her blue-green eyes sparked with anger, but that very energy called to him as it had that night. Damn.

He grabbed her by the shoulders to push her away, but instead, pulled her toward him, his mouth descending.

"I heard Macy was foaling. How's it going in—" Cole's voice stopped him cold.

What the hell was he doing? He dropped his hands from Jenna and stepped to the side, ignoring the surprise in her face. "It started out sticky, but Dr. Jenna got the mare back on track. They're bonding now."

Cole, still in his fire department t-shirt, looked at him then at Jenna then back again. He must have just come home from his latest shift. What timing.

Logan's cousin frowned before retuning his gaze to Jenna. "Were you leaving? I'd like it if you could check on them in a bit. Could you come inside for a cup of coffee?"

She faced Cole. "I would be happy to if you could switch out that coffee for a beer. It was a little nerve-wracking there for a while."

"Of course, whatever you want." Cole opened his arm toward the ranch house, but after Jenna walked by, he shook his head at Logan before following.

Logan could hear him as they walked away. "I hope Logan didn't get in the way. He can be hardheaded at times and that foal is important…"

He fisted his hands to keep from running after them, mainly because he didn't know if he could keep himself from punching Cole or kissing Jenna. Either action would cause a hell of a lot more clean-up than he was willing to commit to, so instead, he strode outside and around to the side of the barn where Black Jack was housed beneath a roof, but with just a steel pipe fence to keep him in.

The horse snorted and moved toward him.

He felt a certain sympathy for the claustrophobic horse. He certainly understood wanting to remain free. "What do you say we go for a quick ride? Then I'll come back and see how the new foal is doing."

Black Jack lifted his nose over the fence.

Logan shook his head, but stroked the horse on its nose, the white star in the middle impossible to ignore. "If you let me in, we can head out."

The horse nudged him, looking for a treat.

"You have a one-track mind, my friend." Stepping away, he moved to the small shed he'd built against the outside of the barn, next to Black Jack's cover. He hefted the saddle from the bench and grabbed the horse's bridle.

In no time, he had the Quarter Horse ready to ride and jumped up on his back. Though Black Jack wanted to head for the valley, he turned him toward the long dirt road that connected the ranch to civilization. The valley terrain was too rough to risk at night. Black Jack had enough trauma for one lifetime.

He had thought he had too.

Jenna followed Cole to the house. She'd made it appear that she needed a drink after helping Macy, but it was Logan's almost-kiss that had her wanting a beer. He'd rattled her far more than the new foal's malposition had.

Animals she understood. People she understood. Logan, she didn't.

As she walked up the steps to the porch, she was thankful he'd disappeared. She didn't want to lose the Benson-Hatcher business, but every time she arrived, if Logan was around, he argued with everything she said. If she didn't know better, she'd think he was afraid of her knowledge, though his concern for the horses was real.

She refused to be intimidated. The horse rescue ranch needed her more than any other client she had and they were quick to pay, especially since Whisper had set-up a trust for the care of the horses. She just had to forget she and Logan had one amazing day and night together.

The house was a bit warmer than the cool September evening. At least the heat of the days dropped below triple digits on occasion now, always a welcome reprieve for native Arizonans like herself.

"I'm sure everyone is anxious to hear the good news." Cole looked back at her as they headed for the kitchen. "We haven't had a baby born here since I turned it into a horse rescue ranch."

She smiled, happy to have another topic to focus on. "The foal shouldn't have any long-term complications from the difficult birth. I'll make sure in a few minutes. I don't want to infringe on the bonding period." And hopefully, Logan wouldn't either.

They turned the corner into the large kitchen. The matriarch of the family, Annette Benson, grandmother to Logan and Trace, and their cousins, Cole and Dillon, greeted her first.

"You must tell us. Do we have a new baby to welcome?" The fit, older woman with pristine white hair pulled back in a ponytail, stood, reaching out her hands in welcome.

Jenna grinned as she took them in her own. "You sure do."

Annette squeezed her hands. "This is wonderful news. Cole, get the lady a drink."

Cole, already at the refrigerator, smirked. "On it."

"Come sit down and relax a bit." Annette pointed at Trace who sat on the other side of the empty high chair. "Give your seat to Jenna. She's worked twice as hard as you today."

Trace laughed as he rose. "Gram, I don't doubt it."

Jenna rolled her eyes at Trace, who since falling for her odd friend, Whisper, seemed to be in a perpetually good mood. "Thank you."

He bowed before moving around the table to sit opposite her.

Cole handed her a cold beer after first twisting off the cap.

She took a very unladylike gulp then raised it toward him. "Thanks. I needed that."

Annette frowned, resuming her seat. "Was it that difficult?"

Trace answered before she could open her mouth. "Macy wasn't the problem. She had to deal with Logan."

His words hit far too close to home for her to come up with a suitable response. Luckily, she didn't have to.

"That boy." Annette shook her head. "He needs a good kick in the pants."

Surprisingly, Trace came to his brother's defense. "Now, Gram, I think he's probably had a few too many of those already."

"Well, he obviously needs one more."

Not sure what Trace referred to and uncomfortable with the subject, Jenna changed it by addressing Cole. "Where's Lacey?"

Cole's face softened from firefighter/ranch owner to totally smitten husband in a split second. "She's on her way. She and Whisper just got back from Poker Flat."

Jenna swallowed the beer she'd just sipped and raised her eyebrows. "Poker Flat? Lacey took Whisper to the nudist resort?"

Cole grinned and nodded toward his cousin.

She turned her head to find Trace frowning. "Yeah. Supposedly, there was a wild burrow there who wouldn't leave one of the guests alone. Followed him everywhere. Lacey said she needed Whisper's help to find out what was wrong with the animal."

Cole laughed. "He thinks it was all a ruse to get Whisper to the resort. My fine cousin here is jealous."

She grinned before taking another swig of her beer. To discover easy-going Trace wasn't happy made her feel appropriately avenged since he enjoyed it just a little too much that she rubbed Logan the wrong way.

Trace grumbled. "Wait until one of the women decide to take Charlotte to Poker Flat, then see who gets pissed."

Annette shook her head. "Being around Lacey and Whisper would be good for her. Maybe she'll discover an interest in music or dance. It's bad enough she's growing up among so many men folk."

Jenna doubted very much that Charlotte would be anything but a tomboy, especially with Logan for a father. She might have a chance at girly hobbies with Lacey, but Whisper was more likely to teach her how to suck the moisture from a cactus than discuss the latest boy band. Whisper probably didn't even know what a boy band was.

Jenna examined the high chair next to her where Charlotte usually sat. When she was younger, she'd had a plan. Go to school, meet the man of her dreams, then on to veterinary school, buy a house, set up practice, and have a baby then two years later have another.

Her entire plan went off track when the man of her dreams turned out to be an avid hunter and her loans from graduate school made it more than difficult to make ends meet.

If it hadn't been for Whisper keeping her truck at Jenna's place and letting her use it when she needed it, she wouldn't have been able to take on the additional ranches she had. Her little sedan couldn't reach some of the ranches thanks to the rough terrain and Monsoon washes.

Lacey and Whisper walked into the kitchen. Cole was already out of his chair to give his wife a kiss and a hug, and Trace wasn't far behind.

The love of the Benson-Hatcher-Williams family just accentuated her own loneliness. Even when she was growing up, it had only been the three of them.

"Jenna? Why are you here? Were there problems with the birth? Is Macy okay?" Whisper's usual bluntness didn't bother her in the least.

"There were, but nothing I couldn't handle. Would you like to—"

Heavy footsteps striding down the hallway announced the newest arrival just before Logan's body filled the doorway, a scowl on his face as he scanned them all until he settled on her. "You better check on them now. It's getting late."

She purposefully looked at her watch before taking another sip of beer. She set the empty bottle down before responding. "I was planning to." She moved her gaze to Cole. "I appreciate the beer, but you're still getting a bill."

He chuckled. "Of course. I just hope you don't charge me extra for having to deal with him." He hooked his thumb toward his glowering cousin in the doorway.

She smirked. "Have I yet?"

Cole laughed, and she rose from her chair.

"Thank you for the hospitality, Annette."

The older woman nodded regally. "You're welcome

any time. Thank you for helping the latest addition to our family arrive safely."

She smiled before heading for the door.

Logan stepped aside and followed her out. She kept her walk to a stroll despite her growing irritation with the man behind her.

"It's been well over a half hour. I expected you to have checked on them and left by now."

That was it. She spun around and he halted, stepping back as his eyes widened in surprise.

"What the hell do you have against me?" She pointed at him, poking her finger into his hard chest, then wishing she hadn't when the image of his naked pectoral rose inside her brain.

She pulled her hand back as if burned and squinted at him. "Do you think the veterinary school I attended wasn't accredited? Do you question the validity of the degree hanging on my wall? Or is it that I simply wasn't a good enough lay for you?" Ah, damn, she didn't mean to say that part out loud.

Mortified, she ignored his stunned expression and turned, marching across the yard as if she could pound out the humiliation of having revealed her insecurity. When she reached the barn, she softened her steps until she arrived at the stall.

Glancing in at the new baby suckling its mother's teat helped calm her. Silently, but speedily, she ducked into the stall and stepped behind the two. The placenta had still not been expelled. She certainly wasn't going to wait for it, not with Logan around.

Reassured the two horses were bonding, she stepped back into the dimly lit barn to find Logan waiting for her at the entrance. Ignoring him, she packed up her bag and hefted it over her shoulder then strode toward him. Her plan was to brush by him without a word, but his hand shot out and grabbed her arm.

She tried to pull away, but he didn't let go.

"Dammit, Jenna." His voice was husky, like it had been that fateful night when she'd thrown caution to the wind and had fallen for the charming, considerate, cowboy—who turned in to the man before her.

"What?" She tilted her head back to look him in the eye. He was too darn tall and too good-looking.

"I—ah, hell."

His mouth came down on hers so fast, she froze. But as warm tingles trickled across her skin and her muscles weakened, she pushed away, shaking her head at him. "No." It came out choked, almost like a cry and she cleared her throat. "No, I'm not going there again. You burned that bridge, buddy."

He stared at her, but there was no scowl on his face. There was no expression either, or another word.

Ugh, the man was impossible. Hefting her bag from the ground where it had fallen, she stalked away. She tried to get her heartrate to slow, but her breath was still coming too quickly. When she reached her car, she threw her bag in the back and jumped inside, locking the doors to keep him out and her in.

As soon as the car revved to life, she backed out only to see Logan still standing there watching her. Darn, she forgot to tell him to call her if the mare had trouble with the placenta. Screw it. She'd call Cole when she got home. Hopefully, Logan also knew about the umbilical cord, but she'd remind Cole anyway. He might not live in the main house anymore, but he could pass the word on to Logan.

Hitting the gas, she drove down the long dirt driveway, watching for animals in her headlights, refusing to look in the rearview mirror again until a second curve made it absolutely impossible to see him.

Once she turned onto the paved two-lane highway headed toward Wickenburg, she finally gave in to the turmoil inside her heart, angrily wiping away the tears in her eyes.

She didn't cry for what could have been with the man who kept their relationship to a one-night-stand. That was her fault for falling in love with him after no more than a day at the fair and a night of amazing lovemaking.

Nope, she cried for herself because as long as he kept a piece of her heart with him, she would never find someone else, and she was sick and tired of being alone.

Also by Lexi Post

Contemporary Cowboy Romance

Cowboys Never Fold
(Poker Flat Series: Book 1)
Cowboy's Match
(Poker Flat Series: Book 2)
Cowboy's Best Shot
(Poker Flat Series: Book 3)
Cowboy's Break
(Poker Flat: Book 4)
Wedding at Poker Flat
(Poker Flat Series: Book 5)

Christmas with Angel
(Last Chance Series: Book 1)
Trace's Trouble
(Last Chance Series: Book 2)
Fletcher's Flame
(Last Chance Series: Book 3)

Logan's Luck
(Last Chance Series: Book 4)
Dillon's Dare
(Last Chance Series: Book 5)
Riley's Rescue
(Last Chance Series: Book 6) *Coming Soon*

Aloha Cowboy
(Island Cowboy Series: Book 1)

Military Romance

When Love Chimes
(Broken Valor Series: Book 1)
Poisoned Honor
(Broken Honor Series: Book 2)

Paranormal Romance

Masque
Passion's Poison
Passion of Sleepy Hollow
Heart of Frankenstein

Pleasures of Christmas Past
(A Christmas Carol Series: Book 1)
Desires of Christmas Present
(A Christmas Carol Series: Book 2)

Temptations of Christmas Future
(A Christmas Carol Series: Books 3)
One of A Kind Christmas
(A Christmas Carol Series: Book 4)

On Highland Time
(Time Weavers, Inc. Book 1)

Sci-fi Romance

Cruise into Eden
(The Eden Series: Book 1)
Unexpected Eden
(The Eden Series: Book 2)
Eden Discovered
(The Eden Series: Book 3)
Eden Revealed
(The Eden Series: Book 4)
Avenging Eden
(The Eden Series: Book 5)
Beast of Eden
(Eden Series: Book 6)

About Lexi Post

Lexi Post is a New York Times and USA Today best-selling author of romance inspired by the classics. She spent years in higher education taking and teaching courses about the classical literature she loved. From Edgar Allan Poe's short story "The Masque of the Red Death" to Tolstoy's War and Peace, she's read, studied, and taught wonderful classics.

But Lexi's first love is romance novels. In an effort to marry her two first loves, she started writing romance inspired by the classics and found she loved it. From hot paranormals to sizzling cowboys to hunks from out of this world, Lexi provides a sensuous experience with a "whole lotta story."

Lexi is living her own happily ever after with her husband and her cat in Florida. She makes her own ice cream every weekend, loves bright colors, and you will never see her without a hat.

www.lexipostbooks.com

www.ingramcontent.com/pod-product-compliance
Lightning Source LLC
Chambersburg PA
CBHW070949180726
48291CB00004B/1207